WHAT
WE
PICK
UP

STORIES

STACY BREWSTER

Praise for *What We Pick Up*

"Many of the small, precise moments of these stories remind me of an updated version of Hemingway's *Nick Adams Stories*—so real and perfectly calibrated you can reach them only through the beats of your heart."

—Sara Guest, poet and editor

"Extraordinarily cinematic, the stories in *What We Pick Up* light up the most vulnerable and compelling moments within families. Stacy Brewster is both poet and film director here. He tightly spins plots that go unexpected places while exploring the way language fails us."

—Kate Gray, author of *Carry the Sky*

"A collection full of grace and humanity that resonates with tectonic force. You'll want to read it again and again, even if it breaks your heart to do so."

—Robert Hill, author of *The Remnants*

In *What We Pick Up*, Stacy Brewster gently coaxes his characters out of their hiding places and, through them, invites us all to do the same—to demand of ourselves a life lived honest and open where we can see and know all of the aching and tender parts of each other."

—Kathleen Lane, author of *Pity Party*

"These stories are full of characters wholly on the page and unabashedly queer, characters who fight through toxic masculinity to find love, to heal, and ultimately, to live. This collection shows us what families can look like, both chosen and blood. I did not want *What We Pick Up* to end."

 —Emme Lund, author of *The Boy with a Bird in His Chest*

"How lucky you are to have found this beautiful collection full of unforgettable characters, each struggling to find their way in a complicated world. These stories explore the spaces between us, our struggles to live an authentic life, and our yearning to heal. While many of the protagonists are queer men, the themes are universal and transcend classification. Brewster infuses each of his characters with such humanity your heart will break on every page."

 —Liz Scott, author of *This Never Happened*

"Stacy Brewster's debut collection *What We Pick Up* is so damn good—rampant with sharp, funny, melancholy narrators burdened by the weight of either not quite knowing themselves yet, or of knowing themselves all too well but unable to shift course. Brewster has written a wonderful book with vivid sensory details that will stay with the reader for a long time to come. A joy to read."

 —Margaret Malone, author of *People Like You*

Buckman Publishing LLC
PO Box 14247
Portland OR 97293
buckmanpublishing.com

What We Pick Up/ Stacy Brewster

ISBN: 978-1-7337245-4-8
Library of Congress Control Number: 2021938575

"Tea Apron Fire Corn Beer Fish" originally appeared in *Buckman Journal*; "Sea Legs" in *qu.ee/r magazine*; "The Delaware Gap" in *The Madison Review*; "Hiccup's Bluff" in *Rougarou*; "What We Pick Up" in *Buckmxn Story Service*; and "Just How I Left You" in *Plenitude Magazine*.

"People Are People" EMI Music Publishing LTD © 1984. "Just Because I'm a Woman" Velvet Apple Music © 1968. "In the Air Tonight" Phil Collins LTD © 1981.

Made In Portland, Oregon, U.S.A

to Jon,
not too shabs

and to the queer elders,
thank you for lighting the path

CONTENTS

There is great tension in the world, tension toward a breaking point, and men are unhappy and confused.

—John Steinbeck, *East of Eden*

Art attempts to transform men's brutishness into men's benevolence. The faggots know better.

—Larry Mitchell, *The Faggots & Their Friends Between Revolutions*

TEA APRON FIRE CORN BEER FISH

1985

With his brother away—hopefully drowned in the creek—Lance preps for his party. How he yearns to inhabit every role: footman, housemaid, valet, cook, and host. Each one a skill he'll hone as long as he lives, long past the time his arms and legs might begin to fail him. He begins this morning by carrying the card tables into the attic, spinning them on their side up the narrow stairs while keeping the legs from flopping out. He is possessed by the spirit of order. He sweeps the floor and frees the ceiling of cobwebs. He pulls down tablecloths, napkins, tea lights, an array of other decorations. He finds his dead grandma's china stacked on a shelf and unearths them from their padded pockets of plastic. He hunts down the right-sized teacups and a proper decanter to serve wine. His first big party, Lance knows he must make the right impression.

Lance is not bothered by the humidity in the attic or the tickle of dust in his nostrils. The heat of this place feels like part of its Southern California charm, like the tall swaying palm trees he can see lining the next street over, like the geckos he swears he sees out of the corner of his eye, darting in and out of the attic crevices as he cleans. Charm in the way Lance remembers the Fourth of July, when his late mother would host all of grandpa's war buddies out back, men fanning themselves with magazines as they drank beer and swapped stories, grandpa himself the pride of the party—his Hawaiian shirt and straw hat, hand-cranking ice cream and quietly absorbing the world from behind his aviators.

When at last he's done, Lance catches himself at the round attic window, looking out at the long green expanse of Catholic cemetery beyond the train tracks. In his mind, the men and women gathered there are not dressed up for a funeral at all, but for *his* party, their flowers for him. Tears well up at the sight of them, their bodies genuflecting in reverence to something deeper he doesn't quite understand, reminding him of the inexplicable speed of his mother's death, the mystery of his own somewhere deep in the future. Then he catches himself, realizes he still has the cook's apron on and smooths it down his chest and belly, a new sense of pride slowly replacing the sadness. How sharp he looks in his mother's old apron, the one with crimson fleur-de-lis repeating in hundreds of interlocking patterns, the kind that hides the more permanent stains.

Once he has tasted the soup and made sure the flavors have meshed, he loosens the apron ties but keeps it on, spinning once, imagining for a moment that he is a girl stepping out of the fitting room with a new dress. He readies himself for arrivals and calls the names of each guest as they enter, dusting their lapels one minute, pouring them tea the next. Everyone marvels at his attentiveness. Only when everyone is seated, nibbling on crudité and chatting with each other, does Lance even look at his watch. Everything's on schedule.

And then it is not. Almost as predictable as the monsoon rains that come each February to Pasadena and yet still catch everyone off guard, Lance's brother Andy seems destined to ruin his party. It is the lower species of man—the apes!—who are always knocking over the candles and setting the world on fire. And his filthy brother has the audacity to invade the attic smack in the middle of the second course, an intrusion of belches and stomps so loud Lance knows it can be no one else. And the strange, violent fluttering in his stomach comes back. His brother Andy, recently turned fifteen, his uninvited rival, searching for baseball cards or silverware, some such thing he can trade for cash and dirty magazines.

"What the hell?" Andy says, cornering Lance with unmatched speed.

"I'm just *playing*," Lance says, turning red, the heat of his embarrassment radiating from his chest as he fidgets and squirms in his brother's grip. "Let *go!*" Lance whines, but he can already feel the eyes of his guests on him, everyone staring, doing nothing as Lance stumbles backward, as words fail him, as all the happiness from a moment earlier drains from his body.

"Having a tea party, faggot? Why you have to be such a pussy," Andy says, grabbing Lance by the apron, bending him backward over one of the cardboard tables as all of Lance's carefully placed arrangements go crashing to the floor. Lance tries to free himself, but not until the wobbly table and all its china collapses below him does he find a way, wiggling out of the apron then scuttling into the furthest reaches of the attic.

"Fucking asshole," Lance manages to blurt out. He tries to circle the whole attic, snake out from his brother to make his way to the steps, but he can't. His brother is too fast and strong.

"Such a fucking pussy," the ape mutters, his lips tight, simian nostrils flaring as he approaches Lance crouched between two wooden beams. Lance wants to die, to be tossed in the open grave just beyond the train tracks, to feel the comforting weight of earth tossed upon him.

"Fucking faggot," Andy says as he slaps Lance's face

and flicks his ears, first playfully then hitting him harder and harder until the big explosion comes, a single punch he lands on Lance's face that makes Lance double over in pain and blood and tears. Andy looks at his own aching wrist as though it weren't attached to him, surprised and then nauseated by the flood of adrenaline in his system. He flees, but not before surveying his destruction with a mix of awe and shame, the broken china plates and the sharp glass of a hurricane candle holder, its fat candle's wick still burning in a blob of wax. Andy squishes this one fire down with his sneaker, yelling at the candle and his brother one last time as he sees the way the wax is hardening on his shoe.

All Lance's guests have now fled to the exits. He is alone and can hardly bear this loneliness. He will have to clean what he can quickly before their father comes home.

THAT NIGHT LANCE HOLDS A PACKET of frozen corn to his face. He sits between his brother and their father in the living room, eating buttered tortillas and microwaved dinner from trays. The three of them watch *Simon & Simon* with the volume too loud. From behind a bottle of Corona their father, Andrew Goddard Sr., looks at Lance then Andy then back at Lance, the wedge of lime bobbing and twisting in his bottle as he guzzles. And after a commercial for Excedrin their father tells them what has been rattling in his brain ever since he came home, since the first twinge of pride he felt seeing his sons had fought: "Boys, pain is a thing you can forget once it's over." He pinches Lance's shoulder hard as he says this, drawing it out for several seconds before a smirk widens. "Otherwise, why would your mother have had *two* of you?"

The Great Andrew Goddard Senior, widower of Franklin Street, seems poised to say something else, his face bearing down on Lance with an intensity so strong Lance wonders if it is being conveyed through telepathy. His father's receding hairline, his nose broken years ago from a fall, the clenched stubbled jaw and sunburnt neck from days laying foundation, or re-shingling, whatever work came to him, all his rough features seemed to radiate with hidden meaning until the show starts back up again and the moment is broken. Their father shrugs his shoulders and farts through his lips. Boys will be boys, his vacant eyes seem to say, and it's the final word.

When the local news starts, Andy is allowed to go back to his room free of punishment. After all, the things broken in the attic, the shoe nearly ruined with wax, they are all hidden now. It was Lance who had to stay put because he lost. Now he was being forced to play all the roles and it wasn't fun anymore: clearing the plates and washing them, preparing popcorn, fetching more beer. And still Lance waits to be formally excused, even after his dad begins to doze off on the couch beside him. Lance had no stomach for dinner but now he eats any stray piece of popcorn he can find, buttery asteroids his father has let fall from the bag.

After the news, a documentary begins. It's 1973, the voiceover says, and a rich teenager named John Paul Getty III is kidnapped in Rome. Authorities say it's the mafia, an attempt to extort money from his oil tycoon family. But the rich grandfather thinks the boy has faked it, kidnapping himself to extort money. Getty Senior won't pay a dime to that little punk! Only the father believes him, proven right when his son's ear arrives in the mail. Lance has to laugh at the crude reenactment they put together, the bright fake blood on the actor's face as he screams.

It is this way that revenge comes to Lance. It will take a few hours to build up the nerve, he knows, but after he and dad go up to bed at last, he catches himself in the hallway mirror. Pressing two fingers to the cobalt bruise below his right eye, Lance finds the courage he needs.

He sneaks into Andy's room, creeping gently as his brother snores away the night. It is tricky at first to get Andy's treasured goldfish in his hand. They slip so easily from his grasp and he must be careful not to splash. He will catch hell if Andy wakes. But he does catch them, one by one. He must hold back a gag as they writhe in his mouth, the way they tickle his tongue before he sinks his teeth in. It feels an eternity to get the first one down, a briny mix of salt and snot. But then it's over. Two swallowed, a third preserved in a glass mason jar full of water.

Back in his own room Lance composes a ransom note, words he cuts and glues from spare newspaper. He uses clear tape for the two tails he has saved, frilly orange things he attaches to the bottom of the note. They blink like Tammy Faye's eyelashes as Lance reads over the note one last time before sliding it under the door. Andy will want to murder Lance as soon as he reads it, of course, until he counts the tails. Until Lance offers him the hope that the third one is still alive, only then will Andy back off. For some reason Lance cannot explain, his brother who has never seemed to love anything or anyone, loves those fish and it will be the truce between them, a bitter silence that will at least stave off the inevitable, two brothers destroying each other the way they do in fables.

2016

Lance checks the weight of his propane tank and tests all the burners on his grill. He sets places at the table outside. He's come across a simple elegant recipe; one he hasn't made in a long time. Dry-rubbed salmon in tinfoil canoes dressed in tomato, dill, lemon, and garlic. For a side dish, ears of corn with their angelic hair plucked out, then the cobs brushed with a mix of butter and Sriracha but still attached to their husks so they can go directly on the grates. All of this easy to prep ahead of time. As everyone finishes cocktails, Lance can throw everything on and his perfect dinner for eight will be ready in a flash.

Lance is in a good mood. When he looks at his phone, there is a new email from his brother with a dramatic subject line, but Lance refuses to read it. Not yet. He doesn't want any tremors of bad news, the faintest ripple in the pond, to ruin his party. Andy's visiting their sick father in Vegas now, helping clear out the condo and move him to a home. A thousand-plus miles as the crow flies from Seattle, yet they are still invading his thoughts with their little armies.

Lance opens the outdoor fridge to stuff his creations in. Satisfied that everything's in order, he pushes the silver tray of salmon in, but it won't fit until he pulls out a bottle in back—a single Corona, the remnant from some pool party only god knows when. It's not a beer either Lance or his husband drink. Still, Lance pries off the cap and downs enough to make himself belch. The beer is nearly skunked, but ice cold and refreshing just the same.

Lance wipes his hands on his apron, one of several gifts his brother Andy sent when he and his newest wife could not come to the wedding. It says *Mr. & Mr.* in giant cursive above an official looking crest of arms that had only Lance's last name. Lance can't be certain, but he's sure it's the kind you get from a special catalog. All the various combinations are there for you, you just fill in what you want it to say. Never mind that he didn't know that Lance took his husband's name, that he was no longer a Boyles but a Boyles-Garcia. Still, even if it was his wife that ordered it, it was thoughtful, almost shockingly so, a glimmer of hope that when brothers have the kind of distance between them they did now—at opposite ends of I-5, practically in separate countries—they don't spend their days plotting revenge.

Now he has missed two calls from Andy, received three cryptic texts urging a call back. Lance wishes he had the energy to call him, but he is not the Super Adjusted Gay who can host a party with his intentional family while summoning the focus to deal with his biological one. He can't double-dutch with his brother's moods, his bloated sense of martyrdom for all he does to take care of their father. A quarterly field trip from San Diego to Vegas, where Andy spends most of his time gambling, is not worthy of a medal. It was a year ago, when he and Andy made this arrangement about who would do this work. Dad had clung so closely to Andy and ignored Lance, that when the brothers said goodbye, the idea that Andy would be the one to manage dad's move and sell the condo was another silent deal between them, the kind only brothers know how to make, hugging not for love but to peer down each other's back to compare scars.

Lance switches gears, abandoning the prep outside to grab the water boiling on the stove inside, a vat of loose tea with herbs, spices, and dried bits of peach he's begun to sell at the Capitol Hill's farmer's market, something new to slap his restaurant's label on. He strains it into a glass carafe filled with ice. The smell reminds him of sun tea he used to make and he ladles some into a cup to taste. It's not quite there, the honey sweetness outmatched by the copper tannic bite of over-steeped leaves. He squeezes in more honey and stirs.

Music pours out from speakers inside and outside; a small feat of technological prowess Lance feels wholly detached from. It's his husband's thing. Lance can handle the volume but doesn't know how to change the music without messing everything up. His vision of their party involved jazz, or maybe something more bluesy— harmonica, banjo, bass—but he knows everyone will like the '80s Britpop and New Wave that's playing now. Lance sings along to Depeche Mode.

People are people, so why should it be, you and I should get along so awfully?

How his dad had been so confused by that song. "What do those words mean?" he'd blurted out one school night, drifting past the doorway to Lance's room then stepping back to linger, face squinted, listening to the song then repeating the lyrics aloud as he heard them, his words garbled from the roasted peanuts he popped in his mouth: "'Takes another man?' Is that a fucking homo thing?"

He may not have said it quite that way, but it's what he was getting at. Lance was listening to pussy faggot

Eurotrash music, music that would turn him gay.

"*Hate* another man. He's saying, 'I can't understand what makes a man *hate* another man,' dad. It's about *bigotry*," Lance had said, surprised that he even dared mutter the words, the kind that would get chewed and spat back at you in that house, spun into something about which their father was victim, like his own day-labor jobs being stolen by *those people*. Lance imagined the chores his defiance would earn him, but his dad only grunted something incomprehensible and went back downstairs. Lance's father had left it alone but Lance would hear those lyrics the wrong way the rest of his life.

Lance and his husband's first date was at a Depeche Mode concert, the summer of 2001. A mutual friend with extra tickets had been wanting to set them up for months but Lance had resisted for one primary reason. The man his friend was setting him up with was also named Andrew, same as his father and ape of a brother. How much extra time had it taken to fall in love with *his* Andrew—Andrew Manuel Garcia—to see a future in those two honey brown eyes that sat like candied ginger above his perfectly trimmed beard? Six months? A year? How long before he was charmed by how shy this new Andrew was, up until the moment the DJ played music he liked, at which point his whole body became a possessed thing, a sweaty voguing goddess? How long before his Andrew grew nicknames, became Lance's dancing bear, his *Drew*, so that the other Andrews were forgotten. Forgotten when he kissed Drew's lips or bit his nipples, forgotten when he sucked his cock.

And now they were together. Now they were *husbands*, by god. *Fathers*. Something neither of them had grown up and seen coming, the dignity of it, the possibility that their bodies might be safe from harm, even worth something. Not the diseased lonely future Lance was brought up to believe was his inheritance. Not Drew's future either, his parents' fears mixed with his, which were fixed on eternal damnation, all of their fears intertwined in that house full of candles that he spent most days locked in his room instead of playing with other kids. Now his Drew was out walking their Boston terriers, finishing a long to-do list that included lighting candles inside hurricane holders, sparking incense, getting the music going, and after all that, walking their son Marco up to the neighbors so he could spend the night. They were so proud he had a gaggle of friends to make a fort with, the kind with only room for them and the television, microwaved popcorn, and their favorite old movies they'd been watching on a loop every weekend since school started, the *Back to the Future* trilogy.

Their guests will be three other couples, friends they have only seen in dribs and drabs in the years since they adopted Marco—for brunch dates, at a fundraiser, or too briefly at Lance's restaurant. Away from these friends like this, the world has gotten too precious, too focused on safety. He feels out of practice with dirty jokes, has not smoked pot in over a year. He has forgotten what it is like to be spontaneous, to let the night happen as it will despite his plans. Sam and Amrit, Chris and Justine, José and Will, they'll all make his cheeks ache from laughter. They will tell old stories and get him drunk and high and giggling. And long afterward, Drew will come back to their room with a second wind, the two of them horny as caged bulls.

When the doorbell begins to chime, Lance sets the burners on high, scrapes the previous week's crust off the grates, then returns them back to low, watching the orange flames flare then simmer to blue. He can hear someone howl with laughter inside, hear the bossa nova rhythm of Drew shaking the first cocktails. Lance waits. He lets his absence be felt. He takes a final moment to rearrange the flowers on the table—peonies and ferns and roses. How he still craves to play all these parts—footman, housemaid, valet, cook, and host. How he loves the little details, no matter the time and effort it costs him.

Lance decides to check his brother's messages after all, holding the phone to his ear as he finds the Corona he left by the grill. His initial buzz has dissipated. The beer is too warm now and he pours the rest out in the sink as everyone begins to spill outside. He simultaneously hears his brother's words that their father is dead and, instinctively, waves hello to each of his guests, missing some of his brother's words, then hearing them again when he replays it. He can picture his father collapsing. The massive coronary that stopped his heart. Andrew Sr., clutching his chest as he strolls from the air-conditioned bliss of a dark casino into the blinding heat of a midday Vegas sidewalk.

Lance puts the phone in his pocket, then moves to wash his hands one final time. He smells something in the pores of his skin or perhaps it is only lingering in the drain, a mix of iced tea and beer, corn husks and salmon. There is a violent spasm of butterflies in his stomach, nausea as his body grows light and tingly for a moment. A diaphanous screen is being pulled across, separating Lance from where everyone is visiting on the patio. His father is dead and Lance is still sober. He feels a sudden sense of shame. The meal he's prepared is inadequate, the tea over-steeped, his clothes uncomfortably tight and stinky. He will be unbearable trying to hold this all in tonight, a mix of crabby and silent. Lance registers the look of concern in Drew and recovers as best he can, shaking it off, smiling and waving each one in for a hug. For the briefest of moments, he flashes on his brother, the attic, a fist fight, and he is shocked at his own desire to call Andy right away.

"How is your son?" Amrit is saying, squeezing Lance's shoulders too tightly, and then Justine chimes in as well, "Yeah, what's that handsome devil Marco up to?" but Lance can only think of his father, has to will himself not to shout the words "He's dead!" for fear of how those words may set the house on fire. No, only Andrew can put these pieces together. "He's at a sleepover," Lance says, finding his smile again, finding his charm. It's so willful, this amnesia. Only the right combination of words can make old pictures emerge from the noise before they're plunged back under again.

2045

Lance's nurse prepares his bath. He hates bathing like this, but it is the only way to clean up properly for a party, especially his last. There is always the scent of something in it though, lavender or chamomile, that makes him feel as though he is the one being steeped, that he is the tea that will be sucked down to the nibs and discarded.

He envies this young man's strength. He can see it all in the mirror, those two muscular arms poking out from his scrubs, the arms that cradle Lance's armpits to ease his naked body into the tub. He hates that look of serenity in the nurse's eyes, as though Lance's freckled flesh and shrunken penis, his gray pubic hair, are all part of a day's work. It will be a relief for this young man when it's all over, won't it? When Lance is dead and he can move on to someone else, someone less irritable than he has been these last few months.

During his bath Lance's mind drifts to his party, the weight of it. All the roles he loved to play—footman, housemaid, valet, cook, and host—have now been outsourced. A privilege of old age or admission of weakness? Lance isn't sure. His restaurant is handling the food. His son Marco and daughter-in-law Lynette will host, greeting everyone as they arrive, making sure everyone has a nibble of this or that, a cocktail. Lance still refers to their son, his grandson, as Baby Drew, although he is grown now, over six feet, and a high school graduate as of last Wednesday.

Some of Baby Drew's friends have brought their instruments tonight. Bass, banjo, harmonica. They play old-timey folk music Lance adores and he has taken some of the good pills to ensure he'll be able to stay up late enough to enjoy everything. His legs have weakened and there are twitches every now and again in his hands, but his arms still feel strong and Lance, with the same twinge of pride at surviving war, looks forward to the later portion of the evening, when he and his son will hand-crank strawberry ice cream from the back porch. If only he had a pair of aviators like his grandfather used to wear.

The young nurse helps do the things Lance's fingers can not always manage: the shave, the pomade, the cufflinks and bow tie, even fidgeting the pocket square into place.

"How does the food look?"

"Delicious," the nurse says, pressing each button of his shirt through, "That's your restaurant, isn't it?"

"Yes. Tell me, what is everyone drinking?"

"Cocktails mostly. An older gentleman brought kegs of beer."

"My brother. Do you like beer? I can't stand the stuff anymore."

"I like it okay." The nurse looks down at his own chest vainly, as though to gauge its size and appearance on a summer beach.

"Do you have one you like?" Lance asks, embarrassed by his own flirtatious tone. When had he turned into one of these old pervy queens?

"My wife likes to drink Corona with a wedge of lime in it, but I hate those. They always taste skunky to me."

"It's the clear bottles. They let in too much sunlight."

The nurse retrieves Lance's cane and helps him stand. Catching himself in the mirror, Lance touches the puffy sac of skin beneath his eye, pinching it around like clay, unable to smooth the wrinkles. He still marvels at the constellation of sunspots on his face, his rough grey beard, his corpse in the Valentino suit like that of a fashionable if somewhat forgotten designer.

"Baby Drew is in the cottage, yes?" Lance asks, heading for the stairs already.

"Do you want me to get him?"

"No, I'd like to head there myself."

The nurse lets Lance make his own way down the back steps, bypassing the kitchen and cutting through the garden to avoid running into anyone yet, letting his absence from the party be felt. An old trick.

Chinese lanterns strung between branches in the yard bob and sway in his periphery. He can hear the walla of chatter down there and, inside, the thumping rhythm of a music to which he has grown unfamiliar. The nurse guides his elbow with a light touch as they traverse the gravel path. Youthful laughter echoes inside the cottage.

The banjo player answers the door. How fine this young man dresses! Blue gingham shirt, linen blazer and pants to match, stunning shoes polished to perfection. "Sir, what an honor."

"I'd like to have a word with Drew if I may."

"Come in," Banjo says, his smile wilting into confusion when he sees the nurse.

"Tell me your name again, banjo player."

"You remember what I play! It's Alejandro, sir. Alejandro Correa."

More laughter in back. A look of embarrassment from the other young men surrounding Drew as they spread and reveal him, shirt off, squatting in his boxer briefs in the empty claw foot tub by the window. There is a new bright flame of blond hair on Drew's head, a stark contrast to his unblemished brown skin. His hair is yellow as corn and pokes out in clumps in every direction. Drew's lifelong friend—now girlfriend?—Sunhwa, the only young woman in the room, stands behind him covered from neck to shins in a vinyl apron. Her gloved hands massage, let the bleach suck the color out.

"What do you think, Grandpop?" Baby Drew says, a grin spreading across his face.

"I think your father is going to chew your ass, young man, but you do you."

"It stings!"

"Pain is a thing you forget when it's over," Lance says, then feels his legs begin to quiver, a lightheadedness that spreads across his temples. He finds a chair to sit down.

"Something wrong, Grandpop?" Drew says, looking from Lance to the nurse, as though beckoning him to inject Lance with something. "Does he need help?"

"I'm not deaf, young man. And don't go soaking in that bath all day or you'll wrinkle."

Drew and Sunhwa look down as though to make sure they really are in a dry tub. Drew gets out and Sunhwa bends him back under the spout to rinse out the excess chemicals. The young men sit together on an open bench at the foot of the bed as she dries Drew's head with a towel. The quiet that spreads over the room is so acute Lance believes he can hear the fizz the bleach is making as it sucks the color from his grandson's hair. Even outside the party has seemed to fade, replaced with crickets and frogs, nature blossoming into a rich bright sheen of sound.

Drew steps into the bedroom to change and Sunhwa piles the heavy hairdresser's apron in the tub, snapping off her plastic gloves. She does her thing indifferent to the room of men watching her, releasing her bun of long black hair, tweaking the bra beneath her dress, a cream sateen with a crimson pattern running diagonal across the bottom, what looks to Lance like a fleur-de-lis.

"Let me see that dress," Lance says and the confident girl—definitely the girlfriend—smiles and steps to him, her bare feet leaving perfect watery prints on the floor.

Lance holds one shaking hand out to it, seeing that it is not a flower pattern at all, but koi fish.

"Drew adores fish," he says, hovering his hand over the pattern of her dress, as if searching out every creature in an aquarium.

"Tell him again how much you like his hair," she whispers. "He worships you."

Lance coughs, his throat tight and parched. On the table beside him is a red plastic cup he picks up to take a sip, coughing more from the malty froth of beer. Everyone in the room is drinking this stuff now, he realizes. The nurse moves quickly to get him some water while there is another knock on the door.

Lance assumes the room is about to be filled with a dozen more young graduates to be celebrated, a cue for him to leave. But when one of the young men opens the door, it is Lance's brother standing there. Andrew the Ape, calmed and tamed, now simply Andrew the Elder. Andrew is alone, the single porch light reflected off his bald head. With both of them straddling seventy, three and a half years seems like no difference at all in their ages. His brother holds something large and round covered in black cloth.

"Well, there he is," Lance says, recovering from his cough. "One more Andrew and the room might explode."

Polite laughter as Lance's older brother smiles shyly and steps in. The charcoal suit he wears looks sharp. There was a time after chemo when Andrew had lost too much weight and would have looked sunken and frail in a suit as broad shouldered as that, but now he was filling it out. Now his cheeks and nose were glowing red again. Lance and his brother had to find their appetites again, slowly, that year not so long ago in which they lived together. It was after his husband Drew's death in Barcelona. And it had been the first time since they were children, knocking around the same house. Andrew had decided to settle in Seattle for good after that, finding a job as a docent at the aquarium, but the kinship between them still felt new, awkward.

"How are you Lance? It's good to see you."

"You brought the beer I hate, Andrew, but I'll forgive you. You look fine in that suit."

"Uncle Andy!" comes a voice from the bedroom.

Baby Drew commands the room in his navy tux, a goldenrod pocket square and bowtie to match his willfully bright new hair. He stands facing the two brothers, looking quizzically at the mound under his uncle's arm.

The older Andrew rips the cloth away to reveal a fishbowl, two glistening beauties in blue and gold dancing in circles, chasing all the light in the room.

"They're beautiful," Baby Drew says.

"I thought you might like them."

"Andrew," Lance says, "they're stunning."

There is a stillness in the room as the heavy bowl of water is passed from arm to arm, from one Andrew to another, as the fish are suspended in air, admired, then placed upon a table.

Lance coughs again, not because there is something in his throat but because he feels the need to separate himself from the painful beauty that emanates from the twilight of the room. A jumble of adjectives suddenly compete for the attention of all the nouns in his head: the wheaty beer, the orange Koi fish, the girl's heavy apron. There are other words there, too, though they elude him. Something missing, something out of order.

His brother places his hand on Lance's back, rubbing it softly then squeezing his shoulder, a gesture so common and tender that no one in the room notices it but Lance. There was never such intimacy between them as adults, even that year living together. It is a gesture that communicates much further back in time to when they were children, the weeks after their mother had died.

Lance feels all the lines of time intersecting. It is not the medication, not even the alcohol, but a sense of falling slowly, as when his earaches bring on vertigo. He grips his brother's hand on his shoulder to hold himself steady, waiting for the world to catch up. He knows somewhere in the dark recesses of his brain there is a combination of words he can summon to make his old life and the days with his husband come back, or those years with mother, certain precious bits he can replay for an instant, however painful. Those *words*, though, what are they? Even if all they did was bring back these last few minutes, he'd make them his mantra. He'd keep circling them, like the fish in that bowl, repeating them over and over and over again to keep the moment swimming.

EARTHQUAKE WEATHER

The day of the accident I wake with my head heavy as a tank. I have to parallel park it between two velvet couch pillows so my back doesn't spasm and I can muster enough strength to tighten my abs and sit the hell up. Dry tongue, chapped lips. The scent of something raw in my pits and in the valley between my breasts, like sherry coming up again.

We're alone. Eddie's father Brian is at the apartment in New York, has been for months. I can picture him propped up on that stupid giant pillow, the one he hugs all night so he doesn't get acid burn in his esophagus, watching highlights from the Olympics as the sun spreads its orange hue across that cold, corporate two-bedroom, twenty flights up overlooking Lincoln Center.

27

Tension in my right jaw, like the words are still clacking in my teeth from last night's fight. It's been months but I can still feel his grey buggy eyes on me when we argue.

We bought this house when Eddie was little, a charming villa some screenwriter owned in the old studio days, worth god-knows-how-much now. Hand-painted tile. Iron railings, sconces, and chandeliers. Curved doorways that help circulate the breeze when certain windows are open. Always the faint odor of dust, or chlorine from the pool outside. A house that spooks me easily, always sneaking up on me—creaking where it shouldn't, vibrating the curtains when the windows are shut, or sloshing water in the pool as though there's just been an earthquake.

Our nanny knew it before we moved anything in. She looked around, got a feeling, and quit. We never replaced her. Eddie has grown up a free spirit. For years the only food in the house has been what his dad or I brought home from set. We could call ourselves Bohemian, but really it's embarrassing how little we know.

Eddie spends these long summer days with his friends. These boys operate independently from me. I rent them gory movies. I order pizza and give them cash to pay the man. They walk themselves to Larchmont to get candy. They pull oranges from the tree in back and pry them open with their unclipped fingernails. They occupy themselves for hours at the pool with barely a burn. If I emerge from my room, I can find evidence of what they've been up to—discarded flip-flops by the TV, piles of wet trunks and towels in the sunroom, empty bags of tortilla chips, the pico gathering flies on the patio. Still, they are young and compliant if I tell them to clean something. Their bloodshot eyes obey and their pruned fingers get to work. They pile sleeping bags in neat little rows for me in the den. I make them popcorn for the night's movie, but one by one their heads droop and succumb to the day.

But not last night. No sleepovers, just PJs and bed, pecks on the cheek and the old routine while I can still get it. "I love you darling," Eddie says sharply, like Cary Grant, "more than words can say." And I reply like old Katherine Hepburn, wobbly and vibrato, "Why tha-t's sim-ply im-poss-ib-le de-ar."

I feel instantly better the moment I've switched out his light. Survival measured in days. Then I do rounds. I check every lock and window latch, that the porch lights are on, that the refrigerator door is securely shut. If I'm near the end of my scotch, nothing but ice to chew, I pull my feet up beneath me on the couch in the sitting room. With everything off, I'll watch the turquoise glow of the pool outside. Most nights this is how it goes, but last night the phone rang and I had to grab it quickly to shut it up so Eddie wouldn't wake. And of course it was his dad, the day's frustration heavy on his breath. The fight began right there.

I made patterns in the velvet couch cushion, fanning my hands across it. "What does Christine tell you?" he kept repeating, trying to triangulate something. Oh god, an intervention. "She says the same thing. You're going to kill yourself and then what?"

THE MORNING OF THE CRASH my nails clink against a bottle hidden beneath the pillows. Just a small sip of scotch sloshes inside as I pull it out. It comes slowly, like good wine with legs. It drips one lick of fire on my tongue, two licks, and I let the lava sludge down easy, burning my neck, swallowing to feel my brain come alive at last.

The first real sound this morning is Eddie's cereal bowl in the kitchen, each metal clang like bolts of electricity in my forehead. The G.I. Joe song is on the television which is how I know it's between eight and nine, that it is still summer 1984.

That's it, isn't it? The Summer of the Los Angeles Olympiad. That's why the energy's so off. Everyone evacuated before the Games. An eerie stillness has taken over—on the main roads, at the Beverly Center, at restaurants that don't need reservations anymore. Last weekend we watched runners carry the Olympic torch along Rossmore, but that was the last crowd we've seen in days. Did something happen? G.I. Joe's still playing wargames with Cobra Commander so the networks are still broadcasting, a good sign. And Saturday morning cartoons means it's still Saturday—shit!—which means Eddie and I have art class at ten.

I can do this. I can get up.

Except I can't. The tremor's back in my left hand, a slight twitch and a weakness in the muscles all the way up to my elbow. It's been here before, but I didn't really take stock of it until last week, as we watched that jocky little woman gallop by us with the torch. Eddie and everyone were clapping and I was doing what actors do—watching people and stealing little movements. Playing the role of runner in my mind. Feeling the strength in my thighs, the grip of the torch held slightly aloft with my left. Only I couldn't make a fist. My fingers felt only a painful vibration and they wouldn't bend.

It's hard to stand only because I'm afraid to stand until the tremor subsides, lest it spread to my whole body. A director I knew had Parkinson's. He told me one of the tests is to try and walk on your heels because you won't be able to if the disease has progressed. So I walk that way out of the sitting room, up two steps to the hall, across the house then down two steps into the kitchen.

"You think we finally get to do the mask thing?" Eddie says as soon as I make my presence known.

"What's that sweetie? Remind me."

He is asking me before we've made eye contact. When did he learn that, to ask me a question before he sees my face? Did he pick that up from Brian, that ability to willfully ignore the ways in which I'm not like the other moms?

Fill kettle. Boil water. Three scoops of coffee in mom's

31

silver strainer.

"The mask thing! You pour this goo on your face and it gets stiff or something? Then you peel it back and you have your face inside out. You pour stuff into *that* and it makes a mold of your face. I think. It sounds really cool!"

"How do you breathe?"

"Straws up the nose!" This cracks him up. He is overflowing with anticipation and, I realize, already dressed. Did I sleep through the shower going, him clomping around upstairs? Eddie rinses his bowl and stacks it in the dishwasher like a good boy. He looks up at me, his head already above my breasts, leading me to suspect that in a year or two he will be eye-to-eye, growing as tall as his dad, taller. Eddie notices something above my face. Instinctively I pull my hair back into a bun and turn around so he can't smell my breath. Then a commercial for the new Transformer toy pulls his attention. His little mind is already working on his mask. He's going to take his little concrete face and paint it blue or green and give himself yellow eyes. Or red. Something grotesque I will have to see hanging in his room until junior high and it will pull all the air out of my throat, that warped version of his sweet, beautiful face.

THE SUMMER ART CLASS ISN'T fancy but the place they have it is, out at the Getty villa in Malibu. It started in May and it's been our favorite thing all summer. I don't remember the last time we had a thing.

Brian may be in New York, but his Mustang is here in L.A.. How it goes is every Saturday Eddie and I play as though we are stealing it from the garage for our getaway. We put the top down and ride that wave of wind with our hands all the way to Malibu, singing along to Carole King or Judy Collins tapes, or his favorite, the Mamas and the Papas. We always burst in a little late and windblown and arriving this way makes class feel more alive, more spontaneous. It keeps our energy up, too, because there are some Debbie Downers in there. One woman comes with her daughter-twin, both of them in stiff gingham dresses and giant saucer eyeglasses, constantly showing off their art history as they point pale, unmanicured hands to each painting and sculpture we study.

We don't like them.

We prefer the quiet Laurel Canyon hippie—Kathleen, or Caitlin—who defers all decisions to her daughter, an adorable tomboy with hazel eyes and short black hair that reminds me of Scout in *To Kill a Mockingbird.* Everyone notices the mutual crush Eddie and Scout have for one another. I choke with jealousy to look at them and spend half the class excusing myself to smoke.

Two classes ago, they made their own art museum out of sugar cubes and popsicle sticks. Eddie really could be an architect someday. He has an eye for it. They used Legos and little green army men for a sculpture garden, then stamps of celebrities and flags for the paintings. They looked like Andy

Warhols or Jasper Johns. Scout even borrowed her mother's earrings to make a mobile hanging from the lobby like a real Calder. Everything, even the miniature figurines they used for patrons looked perfect, exactly to scale. We shot black and white portraits with the Nikon I still owned, then blew them up at my friend Christine's gallery and framed three of them, the best ones which tickled your brain into thinking the miniatures were real. I was so proud of the way I hung them above Eddie's bed, too, so perfectly lined up. Until I told Brian about them and he said they would fall on his head or cut him in an earthquake.

TODAY THE MUSTANG WON'T start, so we must make do with my Honda, the Prelude with the tan cloth interior and not a single thing exciting about it.

It's morning, fifteen or twenty minutes before the crash, and I haven't really been drinking. A breathalyzer wouldn't say anything. A couple drops of scotch is a blip, an anomaly. I've come down from last night. The tremor has quieted. I've showered and gotten everything ready. We're not just on time, we're early. Even Eddie's impressed. We throw our things in the backseat, including towels and swimsuits so we can hit the beach after. We roll down our windows to let out the heat, and I start the car to get the air conditioning going. And Eddie doesn't seem too annoyed when I have to run back inside because I've forgotten deodorant.

To get to the Getty Villa in Malibu, you head west

on Third, left at the Beverly Center, right on Burton Way through Beverly Hills, then Wilshire straight to Santa Monica and up PCH. This is the way I prefer to go because I hate taking the freeway—too grey and too fast. The longer way means the streets are lined with skyscraper palms and everything is mowed to perfection. You can watch people jogging, walking their dogs. The flowers are all vibrant birds-of-paradise and the reality is that, on that stretch of road, nothing ever dies.

None of the leaves are brown. The sky isn't gray.

When I booked the Swatch ad last year—me hugging the giant white dog with eight colorful watches on my wrist—I didn't know when the ad would come out or that they would put up so many billboards. After so much nothing, suddenly I was everywhere again, and it sounds awful but I liked to take Burton because there were two of me on that stretch. I'm not even sure Eddie knew they were up yet. I didn't point them out. He's embarrassed by me sometimes. How could I explain to him that sometimes you need your old self to shine through and tell the present tense one things are going to work out?

I want to say for sure I'm not looking up at one of my billboards when the accident happens, that I'm not lighting a cigarette or fiddling with the radio, but I can't. It's all fuzzy.

I had a green light at Doheny. I know that. Why else would the Bronco turn like that in front of us?

I brake as fast as I can.

I will learn from the cop later that reaction time, before your body can respond, is less than two seconds. At the posted speed, it would take another two seconds from the time you braked to the time the car stopped completely. An eternity, no matter what the physics says.

When I tell the story later, I will say the Bronco flew, but that's only because the Bronco is instantly up and over the front us, flipping end over end like Mary Lou Retton on balance beam. Only she fucks up and lands squarely on her head. NBC cuts to commercial.

Then a magic trick as the driver, a young man, escapes just as acrobatically from the upended Bronco. The roof is barely dented and he's managed to get his seatbelt off and find his sea legs in the bed of broken glass. It takes a second or two, but when his mind catches up to his body, he sprints several yards away, as though his car will attack him, or a bomb explode.

Our car is stopped dead. Eddie is wide-eyed, chest pumping with short breaths. A chant like *fuckfuckfuck* exhales slowly out of me, has been since I started braking. My chest aches where the seat belt has dug in. And my right leg is still pushing down on the brake, as far as it will go, unable to let up for fear of what will happen if I release.

I lay hands on Eddie. From the crown of his head to his feet. Does anything hurt? He's shaking his head, trying not to cry but he can't help it. I don't know how I open my dented door or make my way over to his side but I do.

I'm unbuckling him, yanking him out, rubbing his hair, the back of his neck, feeling his chest heave against mine. We stumble away from the car like animals unable to process how our feet make purchase with the asphalt. Time is not like regular time anymore. Cops are already here somehow. The street is closed off with a line of flares. People are outside watching.

I can't wait for machines to haul the car away. I can't bear to look at it, the front pancaked like a toy, like Thor's hammer came down from the clouds. How many inches over until that would have been our feet in there, our legs severed at the knee, every bone on down to our toes crushed like peppercorns?

The cops measure everything for their report. The position of vehicles. The length of skid marks. We are handed blankets and led to seats in the median as though a director is blocking us for a picnic scene.

Medics check our eyes for dilation. They scan our bodies for bruises. Their white and blue uniforms glow in the bright morning sun. Their attention makes me half-expect hair and makeup to come over for a touchup.

They work on the young man across from us, too, three lanes over to the curb, his body framed by the pink apartment complex behind him that pops with purple chrysanthemum. He is alive. We are alive. The young driver stares our way, but doesn't seem to register who we are. I can read his mind. It's saying *holy shit* over and over.

Holy-fucking-shit. If Eddie's dad were here, there would've been words. He would have berated the dumb kid with his souped-up truck, his male bravado, his impatience in making that turn. *I wish your skull had been crushed*, he would scream, or something to that effect, but without the follow-through. He'd threaten to sue.

Eddie throws up, right in the road, right on the streak of black rubber our tires have left. It smells of bananas and something burnt, like microwaved bacon. A line of spittle dribbles on his shirt. I do everything right, the tissue I have at the ready so he can wipe his lips, clear up the snot, the way I rub the middle of his back with my hand. How much of this performance can I get away with?

No one in the crowd that has gathered knows the way I fought with Brian last night, the things I said about his little dick and what I knew he was doing with it. How he took no responsibility for the miscarriage, my misery, or wanted to hear what it felt like that there was no work to come back to, that no one wanted me anymore. I am certain not one of these rubberneckers at the intersection of Doheny and Burton knows the ways I've justified my drinking, not one of them knows the ways it's held the wolves at bay.

They're all watching as Eddie and I stand. I picture them in grandstands as they clap and clap, inspired by my strength of going through with it, clutching my son to me as we cobble ourselves together, as we persevere. They push tears from their cheeks, marvel that no one was taken by ambulance. The sun is shining, no clouds in sight. Life persists! And my god if that's not the lady from that long-running police show on ABC, the one cancelled a few years back. Same one on that billboard right up there. A famous person! Remarkable!

One onlooker offers to let us use her phone. She wears a muumuu—floral pattern, pockets for tissues, fraying a little at the bottom. She has a silver helmet of hair perfectly tight with hairspray and teased to what must be the exact height of two inches. This helmet doesn't move as we follow her, as she uses a magnetic fob to buzz us through and walk us past a tropical jungle of patios to her door.

She lets me use her bathroom first and this is where I finally let go and throw up, one hand holding the coral shag seat cover open, the other gagging myself, making sure to get rid of everything. Didn't matter there is a fan on in there. I know she hears and I know Eddie hears. And I linger there a long while, flushing twice and spraying her orange-scented potpourri so that none of that scotch-smelling bile can be traced.

I make Eddie use the bathroom after me so the woman can't snoop and when I return to her living room, I see she's laid out everything for me. The rotary phone extended to the coffee table, a giant tumbler filled with ginger ale and ice making a fizzy sound. She has even given me the room, sitting instead in a small patch of sun on her patio. I figure this is for privacy but then I realize the sliding glass door is open. I can smell the tang and tar of her cigarette as she talks to me through the screen.

"There's some whiskey in the cabinet over there if you need," she says, lifting her muumuu free of her legs just enough to cross them comfortably. It is so bright where she sits, I wonder if this is some kind of test, if she would even see me take a sip of alcohol in all these shadows. What if the officer smells it on my breath?

"Is there a phone book?"

"Under," she says, gesturing with her cigarette finger so I understand it's under the coffee table. Her gestures are subtle, not too big, like someone trained as an extra. Background talent.

As I reach for the phone book, my nose is so close to the ginger ale fizz, it tickles. It smells sweet and inviting. I could add a splash of whiskey and no one would know.

"I want to call *dad*," Eddie says as he returns, plopping himself down on the couch beside me.

"We can't, tiger, it's long distance. We'll call him when we get home."

"But we have to tell him we're *okay*," he says, voice cracking a little.

I comb his hair with my fingers, correcting his part. "He doesn't even know anything has happened. Don't worry."

"You can call him," the woman says. "I don't mind. If it's short."

"His father's in New York, on business, I don't want

to—"

"I insist," she says, turning her head up and away to take a long drag. Mother smoked like that.

Eddie reaches for the phone, almost knocking over the glass. "Hold your horses. I'll do it." Now I'm annoyed and this woman doesn't know what she's doing, forcing me down this road. I slide the drink away from us and pick up the handset. "Thank you. I'll be quick."

The rotary dial takes an eternity. Is it the tremor in my hand or is the dial heavier, the rotation stickier than the one we used to have? Does Eddie notice my left hand twitching a little? Please don't answer, Brian, please don't—

"Hello?" a young woman's voice alights from the other end, chipper and polite.

"Is Brian there?"

"Who's this?"

The alcoholic ex-wife who nearly killed his son today, sister-woman.

"It's Margot," I say, massaging the lids over my eye, inhaling deeply. "You know. *The* Margot."

"Oh. Well he's not here just now, can I—?"

"Not there or can't come to the phone? Which is it?" I can't look at Eddie. I can't look at Eddie or this thing will start to unravel.

"He left for set about an hour ago. Did you want to leave a message?"

"We'll call back another time." Deep inhale. Place the

cradle back. Exhale.

"Mom!"

"Eddie, I don't want to hear it. He's not home. We can try from the house. *Later.*"

"Who were you talking to then?"

I'm already picking the phone back up, dialing the taxi service advertised on the back of the yellow pages. "No one. His answering service. He's on set already."

After I've told the taxi dispatcher where to pick us up, Eddie crawls into my arms, forcing his ten years onto my lap. I can already see the diner I want us to go to after we get home, the one near Paramount we can walk to, with high booths in back where we can tuck ourselves away, where I could get a beer and the waitress wouldn't care and the steak fries would be incredibly long and greasy, sugary ketchup spiking magnificent arcs in our teeth. Oh, the most wonderful nap I would have after that meal.

Eddie reaches for my tremor hand and squeezes it tight.

"Ow, Eddie, that hurts! Get up. We've got to finish up outside before the cab gets here. Thank you for the use of the phone, ma'am," I say abruptly as the old woman comes back inside. She beats me to her front door and I want to smack her hand off the doorknob, but I don't. She pauses there, a bit too long, staring. She may at last recognize me or think she recognizes me.

"Sure you don't want to wait here?"

"Actually, can I ask one more thing? I'm sorry. You've

been so kind to let us use your bathroom and your phone. Could you follow me back out there, watch him while I finish up with the officer?"

"I can do that," she says, sounding disappointed, looking down at Eddie whose pout seems on the verge of tears. If she asked him, he would tell her all about the masks he was going to make in art class, about the straws you stick up your nose and all the ways he planned to paint it after, but the excitement has already been drained to a simmer, a slow dawning in his expression that we aren't going, can't possibly go. The day will not go as planned. Does he understand yet that none of them do? That no pattern can be read in the sky or the wind to tell you when earthquakes are coming?

Outside, talking to the officer, I am disappointed to learn the young man in the Bronco has already been cleared to leave the scene. He is gone. There will be no fight, no climax. All the information I am to need is on a slip of paper the officer hands me and it all feels so underwhelming without someone going away in handcuffs, without a resolution. "Faulty brakes," the officer says with pursed lips and a shrug and he might as well be telling a story that happened in another world now that the glass has been swept up, the cars hauled away and the traffic opened up again.

"What am I supposed to do with that?" I ask.

WHEN THE CABBIE ARRIVES, I collect Eddie. From across the street he asks us where we are headed, but instead of answering him I ask Eddie about the diner, Eddie who only shrugs.

We get in, our bodies sticking to the hot black vinyl.

"What did the policeman say about the car?" Eddie says to his sneakers as he kicks the front seat.

"Just a second, driver. About the car? What about the car? Sweetie—"

"When do we get it back?" he whines.

What does Eddie know about a totaled car? What does he know but the cartoon shows where cars reassemble themselves into robots then back again fresh as new?

"We don't get it back!" I blurt out.

Eddie begins to cry and through the tears says, "Why did you make us go inside if the policeman was going to take the car away?"

"Because that's what happens, tiger. When it breaks, it gets towed away forever. But we'll get a new one. I promise. It's really okay."

"But—"

"I stopped as fast as I could, Eddie. This is what happens if you're not careful. If you just… You know what? Here, let's eat something,"—I pull the lunches Eddie packed for us out of my purse—"Tell you what…Driver? Would you be able to rush us out to Malibu? We're late for something.

I've got a fifty if you think that's enough."

The cabbie pauses, his head cocked my way for a second but not looking at me, as though calculating the fare or his route in his brain. Then with the slightest of nods, he agrees.

Eddie looks up at me, a hopeful smile now brimming on his small pink lips, snot still bright in his nose.

"We can't let everyone else have all the fun, can we?"

"But it's already *started*," he whimpers. I can see his little head doing its own calculations, that boy thing that becomes a man thing, planning and plotting, which only leads to disappointment, tiger. "Do you think they've already done the masks?"

"I'm sure they haven't. They always start with something boring in the museum, remember? They talk about that for a while before they start the class."

"So we might make it?"

"Of course we will," I say, not sure if I believe it.

The taxi is soaring on Wilshire now. We've rolled our windows down. We don't have our music but we can ride our hands on the air. Hardly anyone's out. They predicted a lot of things when the Summer Olympics came to Los Angeles but zero traffic was not one of them. Maybe tonight Eddie and I will watch some of it curled up with popcorn by the television. Cheer Carl Lewis for the 100-yard dash, Mary Lou Retton on floor exercise, or the lady marathoners because it's the first time they've let women do that at the Olympics. They say running that far is as hard on the body as pregnancy, but I don't believe it. I never believe anything they say about a woman's body.

At the gates of the Getty, the cabbie slows to a crawl. I watch as the driver leans forward, his arms collected on the steering wheel to take in the whole landscaped campus, its coned cypress hedges and wildflowers.

I pay him and nod to Eddie, who bolts from the car and sprints up the long drive, toward the classroom, the first in a series of one-story studios surrounded by gardens. But by the time I catch up, he has begun to panic. The doors are locked, the lights off, and the campus still.

"It's *over*," Eddie says, already a scratchiness in his voice, his tears ready to break again.

"Don't worry. See all the cars parked there? They've gone somewhere else in the museum. Let's find them." I don't believe it, but Eddie does.

Eddie clutches my hand as we roam the museum halls, the Greek statues and Aegean landscapes staring back at us coldly. Everything is as desolate as this Los Angeles summer. Where are the docents with their greedy eyes, urging us to step back from the paintings? Where are the people that tell us where to go and what to do?

Then the sound of little footsteps, a miniature chorus-line of taps on the marble floor.

"Eddie!" a girl's voice exclaims and Eddie blushes at the sight of her, of Scout, her clunky shoes mismatched with denim capris and a plain black T-shirt. Eddie's whole face seems to widen but he is speechless.

"I was looking out the window and saw you come in. Where have you been!?"

Eddie stares at his feet.

"Have they moved the classroom?" I ask.

"There was an accident," Eddie mumbles. I reach for his hand but he puts them in his pocket instead. He looks up at Scout. "We were in a car crash," he says, quietly as though confessing, as though he is about to tell her that his mother's to blame—for this, for the accident, for his father gone, for our tardiness, for his embarrassment at the very sight of me. But Scout doesn't seem fazed at all. "Come, let me show you," she says and Eddie immediately smiles again, following her as fast as their feet will take them.

"I'll be right behind you," I call out, thankful for the wad of tissues I'd stuffed in my pocket from the old woman's apartment. I wipe my nose. Scout's route takes us beneath the museum to a basement with sets of double doors that shut hard behind you.

When I get to the room, I linger at the window next to the door, afraid to go further. All the mothers and students are there, the earnest art teacher, everyone but us in attendance for the final lesson. The light inside is painfully fluorescent and flat. Scout leads Eddie to one of the empty tables. There is something eerie about the scene. No one is talking. Everyone is lying down on long metal tables. I think of medical school and the day everyone must cut their first cadaver. Pop the scalpel in and glide. Pop and glide.

Eddie is unafraid. The teacher greets him with her palm on his head, looking around the room for me, looking for my permission. I wave from the window, a reflexive gesture as my legs remain wobbly. My wave is all the blessing the teacher needs to get started, thank god.

Eddie hops up on the empty table. One towel is rolled up to make a pillow for his head and another is draped over his small chest which heaves in anticipation. They place two pink straws in his nostrils, the bendy kind which he holds and adjusts like TV rabbit ears. Then, slowly, the alien gunk is spread over his face, in and around the small pink straws so that he doesn't need to hold them anymore. The teacher asks him something and he gives a thumbs up. Then he kicks his legs for a second and I think he must be suffocating. I fling myself into the room, but as I approach I can see Eddie's kicking is merely the energy of a boy. His chest rises and falls in normal rhythms, his little fingers keep tapping impatiently on the table. I can do nothing else but stare at those fingers as they twitch and tap. I cannot grab them like I want to. It would embarrass him.

The teacher checks on everyone, and like me Scout is standing watch over Eddie. When I look at Scout and catch her eye, she immediately snaps her head back to Eddie. Is she afraid of me? Afraid on Eddie's behalf? I will her to place a hand on his shoulder, something other than words to let him know that she is there. But she doesn't and I know I am supposed to take charge of Eddie's body, to be the one to tell him he's okay. Because I am the only one who can see him through the plaster. Not Brian. Brian's not here.

My hand goes instinctively to my stomach. I could pass out at any moment. This whole thing could come crashing down, but I force my mind into Eddie's, do that actor thing again. I lean against the countertop and close my eyes until I see it. Not the bad stuff, only Eddie. Only Eddie's face. How his eyes feel pinched, how the weight of the plaster tickles him enough that a goofy grimace spreads across his face. I can feel his dimples showing, the divot in his forehead he gets from concentrating. I can see and feel it all in my head before anyone else can. I can see what his artwork will look like when he's done, after the plaster has peeled from his face, and the mold's been filled with fast-drying concrete, after the concrete has hardened and he's painted it with bright colored glazes.

It's all there, unharmed, if only I keep my eyes closed, if only a little longer.

SEA LEGS

The first night docked at the lake, my step-cousin Julie and I drag our thin vinyl mattresses up to the roof. Our families have been renting houseboats on Lake Mead since I was a boy, but I've never gotten used to the heat here and I can't spend more than a few minutes in any of the muggy cabins. So after dinner, the two of us roll up our beach towels for pillows, lie back, and look up at the sky so bulging with stars that if we arch our backs and look behind us, everything plays in reverse. The stars become the shimmering water, the carved black mesas an ominous, moonless night. And if I stay still long enough, somewhere in my toes I can feel the earth turn on its axis. It feels like falling and I know if I stay this way too long, my nose will bleed. I risk passing out, or falling over, but I'm learning to ride this edge.

Mom won't let Charlie be up here with us. She's told me every way Charlie can roll off and die up here and doesn't believe me when I tell her it's safe. Then again, Charlie can be a pain, filling every moment of silence with one of his tangents.

Julie is one of our new cousins by marriage. She's seventeen, a year older than me, and she already seems so much sturdier, less shy with me than when we first met last Christmas, the two of us buried in sweaters and glasses. Without making a sound or her knees popping the way mine do, she squats at the edge of the houseboat roof, blowing cigarette smoke up at the stars. I envy the way she plays with the plastic wine cup, letting it swing in the grip between her thumb and forefinger, like she has done this so many times before, so naturally, smoking to think and drinking to think. I wonder how much longer it will be before I will mimic these same movements, pretending I'm an adult.

Julie has surpassed me in height and muscle tone since last I saw her. I'm still in transition, still growing, as though every bone, even the ones in my cheeks, are still stretching to find their target. Julie avoids her mom, making sure to always be somewhere else in the houseboat. There's been a fight, something neither of them acknowledge aloud, but it's clear what it's about. Julie has cut her hair pixie short and bleached it blonde. Her nails are all pride colors and she sports three silver necklaces with blank dog tags. All the energy of war is brimming in her silence. And the alcohol seems to have no effect. She doesn't waver the way I do after a few sips. When she throws her legs over the railing to sit, she could be any chiseled, confident boy on my own swim team. She has no breasts to speak of and from behind the moon casts just the right shadows in her lats and triceps. She's even wearing my clothes—board shorts and a tank top with my number in our school colors, maroon and yellow—all of it borrowed because she said she packed the wrong things. For a second, she's Owen, from swim team, his spiked blond hair just two breaths away and no one around for miles. We could—

"Did you hear that?" Julie whispers, breaking the spell. I gather my towel in my lap to cover my half-erection, then sit next to her. Her voice is like a tickle in the air when she says it again: "Listen." But it is only the same soundtrack we've been listening to all night. The laughter of crickets. The swish of lake waves moving pebbles at the shore. Dad, below, with his grizzly snores.

"It's up there," she whispers, pointing to the canyon. Just hours ago, in the thick brightness of day, we could see the mesas clearly from the cove—a narrow beach ending at a row of thick sagebrush, a single footpath hacked up the center, and switchback trails up the sides of the canyon, which now hang around us like blackout curtains.

Finally, I hear it. The braying of a donkey. Violent,

mournful exhalations that echo in the canyon, and must vibrate the lake water, as alive in my ears as if the animal were just belowdecks.

Julie pours the last of the wine in my cup. "Do you think it's happy or sad?"

"I think it's having bad dreams," I say.

"Perhaps it's in love," Julie says.

"Or hurt."

Charlie and I have explored these mesas before. He used to make up stories about the monsters hiding up there. Shapeshifters that turn into crows once you spot them. Small lizard men with octopus arms that could camouflage themselves in the brush and dust. There is an entire arsenal of guns and force-field generators we must carry with us for protection.

Julie and I listen to the donkey's one-sided conversation for a long time before it stops. We yawn in tandem, as though these animal sounds have carried a magic spell on the wind. Julie folds herself into her sleeping bag. I stay up only long enough to cover our tracks, cramming plastic cups below other trash and hiding the cork. The bottle I hurl into the lake. I throw it pretty far, its splash muted and quaint, but I find myself afraid it won't sink right away, that it will bob its way back to us, knocking at the boat until everyone's awake. I stay awake for a long time thinking about the donkey, about my brother, about Julie and her strong legs, her perfect hairless neck, about Owen's lips when he first kissed me, and I wait for the wine bottle. I listen for all the sounds that refuse to come.

IN THE MORNING, CHARLIE nudges me awake with his foot. He is standing between my makeshift bed and Julie's and I think at once how naked I am.

"Go away," I say, hardly seeing Charlie and grabbing for my glasses.

I have taken off everything in the heat, my shirt and trunks kicked to the bottom of my sleeping bag which is, thankfully, still zipped shut. I can feel the awkward poke of my morning wood in the slippery silk pocket of my sleeping bag, thinking first how I must clump the bag around me when I sit up.

"Did you guys *do* it?" Charlie whispers with a cartoonish grimace. I can't help but laugh. Charlie has fallen in with a platoon of assholes at his new school, and these are the kinds of things they have taught each other to say.

"You don't even know what *it* is."

"Yes I do!"

"She's our cousin, dipshit," I whisper.

"She's only our cousin by *marriage*," he whispers back, almost compliant. But when I look over at Julie, I can see what has tickled Charlie's senses, her naked back and arms stretched out from the tunnel of her sleeping bag, a shadow in the corner of one breast visible.

55

"Well quit staring at her, you little perv. Mom doesn't want you up here anyway. Says you might accidentally, oh I don't know, trip and fall into the water." At the word trip, I reach for his legs, but he backs up several steps toward the far end of the boat. For a second he seems to lose his balance and I think he is going to fall, that all the bad things in the world my mom has predicted will suddenly come true. But no. He is not off-balance. Not at all. He is poised and focused as a cowboy. He is reaching behind his back for the super-soaker tucked in his bright purple trunks and aiming it right toward us.

"Julie!" I yell, but it's too late. He is soaking both of us with everything he's got. Streams and streams of lake water hit the sleeping bag I've pulled over my face, and I'm able to look over and see Julie trying to do the same, screaming my name and his and simultaneously trying to cover her chest with one arm. And when I think he's out of ammo, I peek out and get one more blast in the face. I try and stand with the bag around me, but I'm too late. He runs and jumps far and wide, with one beautiful arc and Olympic splash, until he's swallowed by the lake. I am stunned. I cannot even picture myself making such a blind leap.

I watch Charlie surface, already miles into his escape, but I don't stay frozen for long. I squeeze back into my shorts and my shirt and hardly take notice of Julie, holding the top of one wet sleeping bag over her bare chest as she feels around with her hand for her bra. Her eyes are bloodshot and her face is scrunched against the heat. We look at each other like warriors before a battle, our eyes slits, and she runs one rough hand to brush the water from her head, back to front, so I can feel the spray on my face. We score each other with these looks until she brays like the donkey, an imitation so pitch-perfect, so loud, it echoes in the cove and we both burst with laughter.

In the seconds before I jump, I have no idea where our parents are and I don't care. If I were to stop and scan the depths of the lake, over the blinding shimmers of water that gleam like a thousand tiny mirrors, I would no doubt see them. Our mothers in their innertubes, slowly spinning, slurping hair-of-the-dog daiquiris from thick straws. Our fathers somewhere further off, making wake in the speedboat to scout tonight's new anchor spot, another cove of catfish that's far enough away they can smoke joints in peace, sip bourbon from a flask, argue about football and the Lakers' chances.

I hold my breath as I jump, the lake warm and sucking me in with the force of my plunge. I push up from the soft sandy depths and slip quietly into Charlie's wake. I'm not interested in catching up as much as stalking him, the way I do sometimes in our pool back home. Like I'm the shark. He always pretends he hates it, screaming at me to stop. *Paul! I'll tell! You can't pick on me! I'm little!* But he loves it. I spike my hair into a fin, and submerge half my head, commando-style. Sometimes I do the Jaws music but he doesn't really know what that is.

I swim like this, stalking him, as he makes a long arc around the far side of the houseboat. I hope that Julie is there, waiting to surprise him. I've envisioned us cornering him in the shallows, too much for him to squirm free. I feel like we must both have this plan, although we have not spoken a word to each other. But she is not there and I don't see Charlie either. Not until he comes up for air. Not until he makes it to the ladder and makes his way up easily, fist over fist. I'm treading water, waiting, wondering if he sees me all the way out here. I can see the look of victory in his eyes, his thin ribby chest heaving to catch his breath, the lake dripping from his dark curly hair. He sees me, and I watch the way his eyes count the strokes it will take me to get there, to get to him.

In our pool back home, Charlie and I play a form of tag all the time. Whoever is It stays out of the pool and the target in. If you dive in to tag someone and make it, they are It. If you miss, you have to get back out again and reset to the opposite end of the pool. No matter who was It, Charlie would always scream whenever that contact was close, so shrilly it was guaranteed someone in the house would hear. A performance. I expect this now, a primal scream, his jumping in, so we can switch, so he will turn the tables and start chasing me. But he doesn't. He straightens up on his tiptoes. He jumps in place, as though to loosen his whole body, like he's ready to run again, or slice open a monster.

He grips the ladder as though he's about to swing himself into the lake again, but he just holds on tight and leans out instead. He yells: "You better tell her you do it with guys before you try and stick it in her. You better tell her you do it with guys, you stupid—*faggot!*"

I shrink so small not even Charlie can possibly see the blood draining from my face. My palms shake as they circle eights in the water. Somewhere, like the volume knob slowly being cranked, I can hear a speedboat approaching. I can hear our moms kicking their innertubes back to shore. I can hear the brittle shrill of their laughter. I'm small enough now I could get run over by the boat or tossed and drowned by my mother's legs, scissor kicking, scissor kicking, scissor kicking.

I swim to the ladder. Julie is there and helps me.

"They're coming back," is all she says.

"Where is he?"

Julie shrugs.

Inside the cabins are empty. The bathroom is empty. There are closets to check, but somehow I know. He's not there. He's run off. We search the closets and the roof and loop the decks again in search of him, but I feel woozy. With the sun bearing down as it is, I'm sure I'll boil, too, passing out from exhaustion. Then I catch something in my periphery. I see him. A whiff then a cloud, Charlie's circle of dust making its way up the canyon. I don't know why this relaxes me, but it does, as though this is a strategy I can work with, one where I can manipulate which way it goes. Like maybe I can get to him and talk to him before everyone else does, before our parents do. Before they can pet him and run their worrying hands through his hair and ask him what's wrong and have him spill it all out.

When I climb down off the boat to go after him, Dad is there. He is much larger than I am. Already tan from a season of softball, he is dark and hairy and leans over me like the ancient oak in our backyard at home. He smells of baby oil and those awful cigarillos he smokes with Uncle Jerry to cover up the smell of pot—Swisher Sweets.

"Where's Charlie going?" he says, his stiff arm across my chest. He pins my shoulders hard when he's angry and he is so close and heavy upon me I can smell his breath, which is the same tang of his skin, the same coconut on the ashy burn of his tongue.

"I don't know where he's going!"

"Well hurry up and get him," he says, knocking hard on my forehead. "We're firing up the skis and I need you to do flags."

"What about mom?"

"No, you, dipskull. Your mom's driving the houseboat. What's gotten into you? Go get your stinkin' brother," he says and it comes out all sing-song. *Go GET your STEEENKen BROWther*, like he is a cartoon Mexican mouse, or the bandito in his favorite movie, cornering Bogart for his gold.

"Alright," is all I can manage to say to him these days.

JULIE HELPS ME FIND my sneakers and we make our way up the canyon. There is no way up or down but this one, so I know we will catch him.

"Are you okay?" Julie asks as we begin the climb.

"I'm going to kill him."

"He's just a stupid kid. He doesn't even know what any of that means."

"He knows."

I walk in silence for a long time, scanning the dust for Charlie's tracks, seeing if I have the words to say what I want to Julie, searching the silver-brown slopes of canyon scree, as though a word might appear written in gravel, a sentence jutting out from the folds of a switchback, like some timid gecko darting across the plain. But I hope I don't have to. I hope I will see Charlie's face, hidden in the bushes, with his stupid grin and floppy wet hair, excited I've caught him, and let everything else slip away.

I thought I'd been careful. I always locked my door, left the stereo loud, wadded Kleenex in the keyhole whenever Owen came over. Of course Charlie's room and my room share a bathroom. And I can almost see it now, coming to focus on this hot trail. I see Charlie squatting down to his knobby knees by the shower, far enough from the door to my room that I won't see him. He's pressing his cheek against the tile, squishing his face as far as it will go, until he can see something. But it must take a while to fill in the blanks, to figure out why his brother and his brother's friend are standing so close, why they remain glued to the same spot for so long.

"Where is he?" Julie asks.

"Hiding somewhere up there."

"You think he made it to the top?"

"He must have. Where else could he be?"

"I'm tired," Julie says, stabbing the ground with a stick as she hikes ahead of me. "This heat sucks the life out of me." She's doing that thing again. Boy-stomping, tricking my brain.

"You know I'm a dyke, right? That my mom's fucking pissed that I cut off my hair because she knows I like girls."

She stares at me, waiting for me to answer in kind. I've heard her and yet all I can think is how I'm the little kid now and Charlie is the adult that gets away with everything.

"Did you hear what I said?"

"Yeah."

"So?"

"So what," I say. "So you're a *libation*. I don't care."

"A *lesbian*."

"That's what I said. A *lobster*."

"Paul. Listen. It's fun and new and exciting. It's one big inside joke, sort of…secret."

"Until it's not," I say.

"Until it's not," she repeats and we're both looking out at the boats, our ant parents scuttering around to clean up and unmoor the boats from the shore.

"*Liberty*," I whisper, leaning into Julie's ear until she laughs. "*Laboratory, Laaaaaabia.*"

"Liberace!" she howls and bends her wrist and flutters her eyelashes at me, then straightens up and looks at me sharply, nodding her head as if she knows all, as if she sees all. She waits. She watches the blood drain from my face again, as though it is now doing this in cycles. "See?" she says, "You gotta work on that look."

Julie puts her hand at the center of my back, and she holds it there for a long time as we look out at the lake, the glare from its surface faded now in the morning haze so the lake looks rich and dark and deep. She rubs my back in little circles, the way my mom used to do. The way she still does with Charlie. I start to feel that shrinking sensation again, down into the silver curve of rocks where the lizards hide. If Charlie is here, if he comes toward us right now and he's running full speed, he will certainly crush me. Crush us both.

Then, without warning, the donkey brays again, a sound that feels close with us near the top of the mesa. I think I am hearing things, but I look at Julie and she has heard it, too. Just as the sound had cast a spell and put us to sleep last night, hearing it again has broken it. Instinctively Julie runs toward the sound and I run, too, following her the rest of the way up the ridge. The last part is a steep cascade of rocks. We must grab onto bushes, their roots bolted to the cliff, and every few yards of scramble, we slip and backtrack a little. But we don't stop. I can't imagine Charlie has made it this way. He is a tightly wound spring of a boy, but something about this stretch seems beyond him. Like it won't work for him. And now I'm worried. I stop and look back behind me, wondering if he really has hidden from us, if we have walked right past and missed him. Up ahead of me, Julie continues to the top, fisting boulders to make it the last few feet. I want to stop. I want to make my way back down, find Charlie, but Julie screams my name from above. She keeps screaming until I make it all the way up and I see it, too.

My mind plays tricks on me. I see the dark-eyed man standing there, his leathery skin, his pot belly oozing over his jeans. I see him leaning on one palm on a massive boulder as though he is just catching his breath before continuing to roll it somewhere. There is a taste like pennies in the back of my throat, as if something has been rotting up here for days, maybe weeks. Can I smell his breath from here? He is a shapeshifter, one of Charlie's made-up monsters, turned from carrion bird back to human form. He stares at us because he won't need to attack, not at first, because his gaze is hypnotic and we will not be able to resist. This is his castle after all, his last outpost, and we are the invaders. How many feet between him and us? Where is Charlie?

"Where's Charlie?" I yell, and the man straightens up. He stretches his arms to the sky. I grow afraid not being able to see what's on the other side of the boulder. What is the shapeshifter hiding there? Turn back to a bird! Fly away, so I can make sure Charlie is okay.

Julie pokes me in the ribs and points halfway down the canyon.

I see the line of Charlie's purple trunks streaking down the hill, my roadrunner brother *meep-meeping* his way to the boats.

It is all I need, to see that he is safe. Out of the corner of my eye, I see the man move toward us. We don't stay long enough to get hypnotized. We race, instinctively but clumsily, sliding our butts down the ridge, braving the hot rocks that sting our hands, the bramble that tears up our legs. When we make it back to the trail, Julie sprints so much faster. I feel old in her wake, my knees spiking with the pain of gravity, my vision blurred in dust and haze.

At the last switchback, nearing the homestretch, Julie stops suddenly and I collide with her. We nearly fall over the edge of this last low cliff together, a collision that would have tumbled us into a pit of mud and brush. Only her strength and her sturdy legs have righted us and prevented us from falling.

She breathes so hard, she can't speak. She has been unable to speak since we reached the top of the canyon and she points again to the mesa's jutting chin, across the canyon from us. A large boulder juts from the furthest point—a promontory like the bartizan of an ancient castle watching over the lake. It was the boulder we had seen at the top. Standing there still is the stranger. A few long threads of white, almost translucent hair stand upright in the breeze. My stomach lurches in my chest. Then, as if the day has foretold it, like one final spell in the air, the stranger tilts his dark eyes to the sky, opens his mouth, and fills the whole canyon, maybe the whole lake, with the sound of his donkey brays.

I leave Julie and sprint the rest of the way, ignoring Dad and Uncle Jerry at the shore with the speedboat, ignoring Julie's mother Kim sweeping the fire pit. I wade in the shallows and climb onto the houseboat, which is already alive, its engine warming up. The houseboat is unmoored and churning up its anchor chains. And here is mom coming toward me, down the hall, with so much energy. I expect her to strike or slap me. Instead she knocks hard on Charlie's door. "Open up. Paul's here and I'm sure he has something to apologize for!"

Mom tries the knob again, but the door doesn't budge. Instinctively, I get on my knees and press my cheek to the floor, my one eye scanning the small room. I see Charlie's filthy feet pointed toward me and feel instantly relieved.

"Hey bud, you okay? Don't be scared. We're a million miles away from him now. You can feel the engine, right? Tell you what, how about tonight you sleep on the roof with us. Mom says it's alright. I'll make sure you don't fall off. We need you up there, little man. You know all the constellations."

Mom nudges me with her foot to get my attention, then starts to kick harder, whispering only as loud as she can so Charlie won't hear. "Who is a million miles away? Why was he crying? He wouldn't say anything." She grips my armpits, trying to pull me up, as though I'm her rag doll, her pliant possession, but it's useless. I'm much stronger than her now and won't budge. So she let's go, reluctantly, and goes to get Dad.

Julie is here now, right by me, like a scout watching for our parents to return.

"Charlie, it's like this," I say, right into the gap beneath the door. "After it's dark, we take turns leaning our heads back over the railing. You ever watch the stars like that Charlie? Upside down until you start to feel funny? Everything spinning so hard it makes you dizzy?"

The houseboat is now unanchored. I can feel it lurch. But it is still quiet. The parents haven't come because they are piloting the ship. Still, the ghost of that stranger and his donkey sounds echo in my brain. I can hear them in Julie's concerned look. And somehow, I know it will be this day, on this houseboat, this sliver of dull light from my brother's cabin. It will be this moment, my bending down in this hallway, feeling alive and clear, as though we are awakening from years of sleep. This is the adventure we've been waiting for, the one about to burst forth as I wait for the light to find its shadows—first his knees, Charlie's two knobby, reddened knees poking through his purple trunks to find purchase on the floor, then his cheek, all dust and tears, pressed to the tile like mine, his one bloodshot eye, all-knowing, all-seeing, blinking back at me.

THE CENSUS TAKER

December 7, 1930

I have done it. Stupid, but it's already done. And I have taken D.'s good boots and Irish sweaters. And the cash he thought he had hidden cleverly in the panel behind the stove.

The trick to choosing the empty railcar is that the door is open. Crates of meat and vegetables stay fresh with all that cold air. So the doors are opened after it's in motion, and there are two switches south of town where it slows down enough you can catch it, if you're nimble, and avoid the men with rifles.

So much of life is preparing yourself to be in the right place.

How did it finally get to this point? Because my money

always runs out this time of year. And a dollar doesn't last half a second in Portland. I couldn't keep it up much longer. The world is a patchwork of remedies and I am a patchwork of body parts, sewn together like Frankenstein's monster.

Patchwork L.

Shorter, though. More sexed, I suppose. Unlucky in all things, but not afraid of fire.

D. wasn't just a suffocating person, he was suffocating me.

And this all got started. Thinking it was me or him. Then thinking of C. and wondering if there was a chance I could go back to Lacomb. Ride the rails from Union Station properly or without a ticket. Last time I had this urge I tossed my bag in first and got clear knocked out trying to hop on. Woke with gravel sticking to my lips and a one-eyed cat, a dirty orange tabby, licking the blood off my arm. Everything not on me was gone forever. That was before D.

It takes a while to build up again. Meanwhile, the country pulls and the city pulls, and the city always pulls stronger.

But Lacomb.

Country Lacomb.

Quiet, little Lacomb.

I kept ruminating on it. And that rumination always ended up the same way. Thinking how I couldn't go back, not ever. How C. would not have me back. How C. was with some other jerk. Or C. had moved away. Or C. was dead.

Then what? Forget about C. These thoughts I would jot by candlelight, late, in a small ledger I've long since burned. So that it was often just me and my thoughts until D. needed it, then Yes, I am coming to bed. I hear you groaning. Yes, D., I'm coming.

The various possibilities have been consistent licks of flame in my stomach these last two months, flame hungry for more fuel, repeating all the same questions.

But those same doubts about the counties south of Portland. And in December! Stupid to try. Stupid to even think of trying. A misery in every calculation.

And so here we are. Inside the madness.

Bailing's done, so there's no farm work, nonexistent these weeks of sleet. The impenetrable hardness of frozen earth. There are lumber mills with their slick, nosy managers who've already trained everyone on the new equipment and not taking newcomers. No latecomers, especially. You'd have to slide in special, on someone else's misfortune, like if someone's been recently departed from their limbs. Patchwork L. could find a way in if that were the case. But that's still rare, isn't it?

Canneries got work, but oh god the rotting fish-gut smell, so much worse than the trash chute at the end of the hall, crawling with rotten cabbage and Mrs. K's rats. Inside, I'm hard as iron most days, but even D. knows I'm too precious for that.

His gloves are a life saver. And writing keeps my blood

flowing on the train. What did Mrs. P. say in class? Keep the pencil moving, children. Keep the pencil moving.

I CONFUSE PEOPLE. D. didn't have that. C. neither, really. No one thinks they're queer. They pass. But me? People can smell it on me. That's why I can't go back there to these little towns where everyone's up in everyone else's face. They know everything and so read me plainly, hearing my every dodge, measuring my contradictions. Those iron insides mean nothing when you look soft, when you find yourself clearing your throat and averting eye contact. Only strangers behave so unnaturally. Criminals and perverts.

In the past, whenever domestics answered the side door, I could sense rooms full of women and girls counting seeds just beyond. They mended elbow-holes, knit socks and scarves, and scarcely looked up when I called, so much tending and attending to do. Domestics sensed it in my eyes, the dim porch light catching the sheen of grease in my hair, the imperfectness of a hair's part that's slightly uneven, done in the dark, on a train, all alone, no mirror. They saw right through me and closed the door on my patchwork face. Repeat, repeat.

Young fathers in Talbot, Jefferson, Whitaker, they sized me up as well. When they were the ones to open the door, and whether it was true or not, they always said they had help enough—or sons, so many sons—and preferred spending those late fall weeks teaching these sons, imaginary or real

I would never know, teaching them something new rather than take on a stranger. It was so close to Christmas. They were saving money for equipment repairs, for toys and other presents, for the cardamom and potpourri they bought at expensive shops in the city for their wives.

But here we are, a moment of truth. I've already risked the rails, will be in Whitaker in less than an hour. It's late, so late, but how hard could it be to walk the miles to Lacomb. I wouldn't need to ask for anything in between. No doors to be closed on my patchwork face.

It has meant starting with a full belly, though. I took it as a sign when D. left his thermoses behind. The big one and the small one. Hot soup and coffee. Adventures have started with less. There was the risk that he'd come back for them, see in me what I couldn't lie about anymore, this desire to leave. But the yards were down in Sellwood. To turn around and come back he'd be docked for being late. Besides, D. enjoyed the camaraderie of the commissary near his work, would find all the sustenance he needed there.

So, food and a fire. Not real fire, but the fire within me for another life, the one with C. I can't let go of. The fire that woke me from a dead sleep before the sun was up, my cock pressing against my shorts so hard I had to free it, quickly, in the dark of the alley downstairs, away from D., spreading my seed to make the fire dim a little, so I could focus on this journey, the desire so strong, even now, to write C.'s name. If I could, it is all I would fill this journal up with, his name in neat cursive, like the census taker's.

There was, of course, the timing of today in particular, when D. was not to be home until eight at the earliest. And a day I was slated to work the bar, another hustle D. had me on, where I take the men upstairs, above A.'s camera shop. Sex that's routine, anonymous, and not quite as lucrative as you would think. And so D. would already expect me gone this late. And he will have brought home F. or T., and frankly would have been offended if I came home too early to find them, all legs and armpits.

D. is not expecting me until morning, in other words. I am hours ahead.

MAYBE I KEEP ENDING up in farm towns and mill towns like Lacomb because I can't cut it along the wharves in Portland, never having learned or acquired the sailor's tongue, their Irish brand of pitch-black humor. Maybe I was too book-smart, too snobby for the grading crews and lumber crews forging roads through the mountain passes. Except they would be wrong on that account. I wasn't too good for it. I love hard labor. It distracts me from everything in my head. Rather, I have a fear of heights, a nervousness down to the core whenever the road spikes up along a bluff or the train cuts its way along a valley you can't see the bottom of. That fear is never hidden on my face. Truth is, what does a kid raised in Iowa City know of mountains like these, of trees reaching so far upward through the fog you can't see their tops, of water so cold and fast there could be no swimming, no period of surrender in this wild country.

When I get to Lacomb, I'll have to avoid the old-timers. Elders see through me quicker than the domestics or the landed men, quicker than I see myself. The untrustworthy, tobacco stink of me, dirt under the fingernails, long fingernails, a quality they hate more than anything—a sign of idleness. The distrust in their eyes whenever they caught sight of me, at filling stations and general stores, at saloons or other card dens. How earnest I tried to look, how innocent and clean. Only I was never able to escape their quick summation: I spelled trouble.

HAVE I REALLY IMAGINED that other world of freedom? Desired it? A world where C. and I would be okay, C. and I would be in love the way we were in love. C. and I would be lovers again in that cabin the way we were lovers in that cabin before.

When the census taker came, that overcast morning April last—my god, it was just April—my answers came so naturally, like we were just any other family. Any other moral, upstanding family. The gall of it. That's the fire I'm talking about.

I can still see the fine cursive of the census taker in her tweed suit.

I must get that story down again. It was in the bag I lost. The one-eyed tabby knows where it went. But it's too cold to write a minute longer. And I've held off as long as I could. Soup from D.'s thermos and pacing as I digest. Whitaker will be here before I know it.

December 8, 1930

I don't know how I know where I am, but I do. I got off before anyone would notice me. The smokestacks of Whitaker were off in the distance and I knew to head toward the rising sun with the hard earth beneath my feet (in D.'s good boots, at least).

If a jalopy comes along with room in its bed for me, I will take it. Migrants are Christian mostly and will take me in back with the chickens if there's room. Thankful for the possibility. Thankful for this sunrise, the clean crisp air. Thankful for no rain, no snow, this calm.

IT'S BEEN SIX MILES, give or take, maybe six to go. No jalopy yet. No anything yet. Still a chance for one. My dogs are tired. Sun bright on this page and I can tell the story of the census taker again while I catch my breath. No time like now.

It meant something that it was a woman. Women understood better than men. Men saw it in themselves and rejected it outright, but women, some women at least, saw in us a kinship, a bit of themselves under the right light.

C. wouldn't let her in so we sat on the porch. Rather, he sat on the porch and she sat on the top step, and I beside her, watching her work.

For the census taker, it was a new line halfway down her page. I could see that spectacular cursive. Not just trained, but as crisp and clear as the air I am breathing right now. Every entry with a sharpened pencil. The satisfying sound of graphite on the page. Her checkmarks. Her numbers. Not a single smudge. I was close enough I could see the headings and her answers as she wrote them:

Name: *F——, C—— M.*
Sex: *M*
Color or race: *W*
Age at last birthday: *42*
Place of Birth: *Oregon*
Father's Place of Birth: *Missouri*
Mother's Place of Birth: *Missouri*
Mother tongue (or native language of foreign born): *[blank]*
Citizenship, etc.: *Yes*
Occupation: *Bookseller*

The census taker nodded distinctly at every answer, no pause, no looking away from her page, no eye contact, no display of judgment or emotion. Calm, deep breaths.

"Married?"

"Divorced," C. answered.

A rare word but she didn't stutter, although she did look up from her round spectacles, the ones I noticed looped deliciously behind her small ears.

And that other word. The one they put by the first person they speak to, the main occupant, the first occupant, the father or patriarch in most cases: *Head.* Meaning: head of household.

Head.

All five senses and the brain. Seeing that word alone on her page, my first thought is that everyone else should be named according to parts of the body. Running legs and bail-lifting arms, sex organs, the cock, nipples that feed the newborns, feet planted to shoot the buck, hands wielding knives to skin it, fingers that press buttons through housecoats to dress the indigent elders.

Except they don't use parts of the bodies. A literal head, but no literal anything else. Tongue, I suppose, but she's left that blank. She's left other things blank, too, special codes she will fill in later. Everything else is relational, still patchwork, still words of lesser than, of subservient to— *wife, son, daughter, mother-in-law, lodger, servant.*

And then she looked up, turning her soft pale features to watch me above her glasses.

What was I to C.? she was asking with that look. How did I connect to the head?

Brother, son, nephew, lodger?

Already C. had gone inside. Any reckoning with government, even soft-skinned spectacle-wearing lady government, made him uncomfortable. Did he remember the last time? Did it remind him of his answers in 1920, back in Portland when it was neatly *Head* and *wife* and *son*. Was there some bit of doubling in this memory of a census taker?

When he was out of earshot, I spoke softly.

"Partner," I said.

There was the first mistake on her crisp new page. She had already written *lodger*. Had she already sized the situation up? Was this the typical language to cover?

"No, *partner*," I repeated.

If she was flustered at all, she recovered well. The pale woman in the charcoal-colored suit wrote it down, forcing the new letters over the word already there so it looked like it had a cowboy spelling, with a 'd' in it. *Pardner.*

Pardner.

The rest of the questions I answered for her easily, the census taker rattling them off with sincere exactitude:

Name: *T——, L—— P.*
Sex: *M*
Color or race: *W*
Age at last birthday: *22*
Place of Birth: *Iowa*
Father's Place of Birth: *Wisconsin*
Mother's Place of Birth: *Illinois*
Mother tongue (or native language of foreign born): *[blank]*
Citizenship, etc.: *Yes*

"Occupation?"

"Worker," I said. "Bucking wood all season on account of his arm, keeping the property up."

Hand, she wrote.

Hand.

So they did use words other than head and tongue for parts of the body.

There it was: the hand to the head. Head to the hand. Pardners. That is, two parts of the same body, connected by blood vessels and oxygen circulating, the nerves firing and animating and making everything come to life.

I could hear the crumble of spent logs inside, C. using cast-iron tongs that scraped the brick as he moved the other logs, a harsh crack of dry knots suddenly releasing their tension.

It was only me and the census taker in the silence that followed, before she gathered her things to leave. Had she thought C. was embarrassed of me? This must happen often with heads of households too busy to stay for the details. There was a sense of finality in the look she gave me, a long inhale with a polite smile. She must have wanted to announce that we were her last stop because she said the words aloud as she wrote them on one clean line, a couple down from my information, writing the words carefully across the many columns: "Here ends the enumeration of Lacomb Precinct." Then she slipped her forms back in her satchel, still clasped to the piece of slate that kept her writing steady and solid, everything now pushed behind her so that the strap of her bag cut through the middle of her chest, hardly registering breasts at all behind her blouse, vest, and jacket. One stern handshake and she was gone.

HAD THAT BEEN THE BEGINNING of the end with C.? He had me packing my things within a week of that April caller, our first in all these months.

"Such a rough and foolish child," he called me after the census taker was gone, but in a way that felt directed past me, over my shoulder, to the mischievous spirits and wood elves attached to the cabin. The sorrow in his words and between his words. The melancholy sweep of him, despite the early onset of summer. Those long days, the tall grasses we could still find surprisingly light and airy as they tickled our nakedness. The cleaving, my departure, so anticlimactic, so quick and abrupt there seemed no purchase in reason, no logic threading back through our silly disagreements that made any sense. That is, other than the most glaring and obvious: that we were destined for ruin the moment we first leaned into our sins.

I AM HERE. PATCHWORK L. HAS arrived in Lacomb. My name and the name of this town, two L's like hooks to hang a sad story on. I am here at the general store and post office once again, the center of all things in all times in all seasons. It is a mad scene, the mail bins bursting, I suppose, full of Christmas letters and the many stories clipped from other state's newspapers. Obituaries and scandals mixed in with the letters, with the crushed petals and drawings of children.

Maybe now I have the proper clothes and boots and my hair is parted in the proper style. Maybe now my mustache tacks on four- or five-years' worth of experience to my measly twenty-three. I'm only a few months older than when the census taker asked those questions, but it feels like years.

A posture of maturity, is that it? Perhaps it is worth something now. No one has paid me any mind.

When I arrived last year, it was so clear I was a stranger to these parts. Shoes with the soles rotting through and the stink of that musty corduroy jacket. No kin to my name, at least not anywhere close. A discardable person, peaty and brittle as the last remnants of fire.

After the business with C., had the folks in town ever wondered about me? Mention me to their wives at supper? Did they ever ponder what happened to that kid up there at C.'s place, cording wood and keeping the place up after his injury? There were always men like me coming and going from towns like these, so what of it? Young men like us got kicked out of the house for drinking too much liquor, for giving hell to our parents, for scarring our baby brothers or getting too hands-on with the young neighbor women, the young neighbor men.

Strangers like us didn't ride the rails out west because of gold or opportunity or any of that old pioneer bullshit, the story went, but on account of us staying one step ahead of the law. Strangers—drifters they might call us—we had smarts, they gave us that, but not enough schooling for fancy careers, a laziness that meant disinterest in messy things and things bearing responsibility. No arguing in court or sewing up a wound. No fighting fires. Definitely not walking a police beat unless you had that itch for violence, which I didn't. Even so, fraternal orders like the police wanted family men, moral types, not drifters who abandoned theirs.

Is IT AS SIMPLE AS waiting here, writing, until C. comes for his post?

C. would have to take me in, wouldn't he? Where else could I go? Otherwise it would be me, wandering the familiar map of the town, it's single strip of shops and saloons, everyone knowing, seeing who I was or beginning to remember. It could spell trouble if C. took me in again, but even more if he didn't. C. is not a natural drifter like I am. He stays put, stays in his lane. Men like C. search for their little pocket to die in and they spend their years living up to that promise once they've found it. Gin helps slow you down, glues your feet to the floorboards. It was only the divorce that spun him out of Portland. What could possibly spin him from here?

He must be here. And he will come to the general store like clockwork, waiting for a response from his son M., the son he writes each week, who I helped him write to, and who never replies.

Returned to sender. That's what he got, over and over.

I'm a little like that. C.'s letter returned to sender.

No mail for me here, but it was worth checking. When last I wrote Mama J., it was this address, the one from last Christmas that I'd given her. If there was cash or gossip or some favorite Bible verse to send this year, she would have sent it here with a prayer. Aunt P., too. Last year, I remember two separate letters arrived, one from each of them, just before the record Christmas storm and two months to the day after I'd written them to ask what they could spare and, if so, where to send it: *L. T———, c/o Lacomb General Store, Lacomb Road, Lacomb, Oregon*—written so that, despite all my other sloppiness and lack of care, that perhaps each cursive 'L' might be a testament to my righteousness, a sense that I'd eased into myself, settled down at least for a while in some peaceful place. Anyway, I wasn't with B. at the place on Lovejoy in Portland anymore. They needed to know that. Just as, after I settle things with C. here and convince him to let me stay, I will truly begin forgetting those other men, those other addresses, the ones that must have their own census histories, if I could ever look them up, at some library of the future. Find B. on Northwest Lovejoy. Find D. on Southeast Stark. See what parts of the body the census taker made up for them.

Then forget them forever.

December 9, 1930

The house is gone. When C. never showed, I hiked there to check.

The house has burned, nothing but its stone foundation and the bases of its two brick fireplaces. No sign of C., and enough weeds sprouting up already, the fire must have been late spring, early summer, not long after I'd left.

The floorboards are gone, but it is easy enough to orient where C.'s hearth used to be. Our bed. And so this is where I pitched my tent, where I slept last night.

I have made my own small fire here, set up a tent with supplies I bought with D.'s cash, something to help me travel west, over the passes to the ocean. It is the only step left. I will find C. and we will make love again at a flophouse in town, one splendid reunification of our bodies before taking him to the ocean for repair—his repair and mine— something to make this all worth it. All we'll need is a rifle, some traps, a sled for gear. I mean it that I'm iron inside, stronger than I look, ready for the hard things.

C. WAS THE FIRST PERSON to lay eyes on me when I arrived in Lacomb last September, nothing but moldy bread and cold coffee churning my stomach after the twelve or so mile walk from Whitaker. I remember noticing the soft-bearded man with just a hint of grey that sat at a table in the corner of the general as I waited to buy paper, stamps, and envelopes. No older than 35, he looked too thin for the army coat unbuttoned and hung over his shoulders like a shawl. He wore clean cotton pants, the same olive color as the coat, and newer looking work boots, dark brown and not too dusty. But he had no shirt on, which was strange, and I could see the brown sworls of hair sticking to his chest from sweat. When he reached for a short glass of clear liquid, I could see that his right wrist and hand were wrapped in frayed yellow bandages, his whole arm slumped into a sling tied around his neck. I caught his eye once but only briefly as he scanned the room. He reminded me of Uncle T. back home, silent and withdrawn from the day he returned from Europe to the day he drowned himself at Sand Lake, that ghostly way he had of looking right through me whenever I played in their yard.

I slunk into an empty table to write my letters and, as I composed them, every now and then I caught another glimpse at this odd man. His head bobbed a little as he looked out the window, a song rattling around up there or, more likely, that drink in his hand was not his first run of gin for the day. Or so I thought before he spoke.

"You ever split wood, boy?"

From across the room, C.'s voice came so delicate and familiar to my ears it must have been a trick of acoustics in that long rectangular parlor with the low ceiling. He sounded as close as if he were seated beside me on a train.

I stopped writing mid-sentence, realizing in that instant how much his presence had been making me uneasy in the first place, an electricity pervading the room so much so it sapped my writing hand, made it feel lumpy and inarticulate, sloppy in the way I wrote and crossed out and tried again to narrate my travels, the hardships and victories I had to get just right in order to win Mama back over to my side.

"You hiring?" I replied, realizing I could speak softly and, by those same strange acoustics, he could understand my words perfectly. By the looks of him, I didn't believe C. had more than a few nickels to his name. Did he think I would be gullible enough?

The years hustling for jobs in Portland made everything transactional and quick. Don't waste my time. And still you couldn't sound too eager, had to play as though you knew you were worth something. I could tell C. liked this, his smile widening so that two pronounced dimples drew in from his beard.

"Only if you can split wood for the entire season," he said. "Almanac says we're in for a wallop straight through March and I'm not exactly fit for the work this year if you catch my drift."

He raised his dead arm up as though I hadn't noticed.

"What could you have going on I couldn't handle?" I asked. "I stocked the entire Harris farm in Talbot last winter."

"Harris! Pfft. That old bag of shit. You didn't work the Harris farm. You're no more than a buck five wet. I bet you fed straw to the horses for the pleasure of sleeping in that ugly yellow barn of his."

I took off my jacket slowly, then rolled up my left sleeve as far as it would go, practically to the shoulder, flexing. It was the only way to explain the odd ways my arms worked, their strange anatomy of power, the muscles strong and taut but not pressed against the fabric of my shirt the way of seasoned sailors and lumbermen. I stood up, taking up the full height of the parlor and crossed to him, holding my left hand to shake his good arm.

"Try it yourself," I said.

With his left hand he downed the last two fingers of his gin, then shook mine, our palms gripped together so strongly, so tightly, it seemed we were both beginning to glow with the surprise of how much we both had to give, pressing further and further until our hands fused together. One pressurized unit. One body.

C. released first and shook his head and began to giggle, childishly so. Then the gin churned up in him so that his head recoiled from a burp and he broke out in a tremendous laugh, high-pitched like a woman's scream. Then I was laughing too, any nervousness or tension suddenly relaxed, already forgetting the soreness in my palm and fingers from his grip. Had there been another soul in that parlor who noticed the two of us? I can't remember.

"I can't offer you any money, just a place to stay. Or were you just passing through?"

"Not anymore. That is, I'm writing my family for some money. I was only going to stick around here until they wrote back. What happened to your arm?"

"That's a long story."

"You fall or something?"

He didn't answer. And wouldn't for months.

"What's your name, kid?"

I told him my full name, suddenly serious, stiffening up.

"I don't need rank and serial number," I just want to know what to call you.

I told him and he told me his name, which was like two first names.

"Which is it, then? C. or F.?"

"C.," he said. "You done with those letters?"

I looked back over at the table, my small satchel still damp from the spot of rain I hit coming in, the chicken-scratch scrawl with all its cross-outs and hatch-marks still waiting to be finished.

"Never mind, you finish up and meet me at Jane's over there across the street. You can't miss the saloon, or Jane for that matter. You look like you could use a bite and a drink."

"I can take care of myself," I said, as my mind counted the coins in my purse.

"No one said you couldn't. I'm just saying no one should subject themselves to Jane's cooking without knowing what they're paying for. Although if your stomach is as tough as that left arm of yours, you'll be just fine."

C. was the first man to ever see the iron inside.

THAT HAD BEEN ALL IT took to make the arrangements. I don't remember the taste of Jane's cooking or the old regulars at the booths. I don't remember the sting of whiskey at the back of my throat or how drunk I must have gotten that first afternoon before walking the four miles to C.'s cabin. They are the same four miles I walked yesterday to find this burned-out shell, then back for the supplies I knew I'd now need. The rows of stone waist-high that served as its foundation are still here. Gone are the clapboard windows, two in front like eyes to watch the road, and two in back that looked out at the forest sloping down to, somewhere unseen, the Santiam River below.

Half-toppled but still somewhat functional are twin fireplaces west and east, their chimneys once like pointed ears atop the bevel slope of the roof, now piles of brick, so porous they have all manner of wildflowers growing in their crevices. Was there anything about the place without such porous magic, without such clean symmetry? The porches front and back identical, running the full length of the house. Front and back door in perfect alignment so that, if you stood in just the right place in the woods behind, you could see clear through the house on a hill and nothing but blue beyond. Even the few things C. hung in the clean, sparse space, little statues and pinecones and knickknacks on the mantle, were like mirror images of each other, so that you could catch yourself looking at one and sensing the world outside the paned glass in your periphery and, for a few seconds, forget which way you were facing.

More than anything you felt its seclusion. It's clean seclusion I should say, because there was never a moment I didn't feel safe in C.'s house that long, relentless winter. What was that about? It was C., yes, but there was so much more. The symmetry? The fur blankets, the fire tended to at all hours? How the boards hardly creaked, the steps he made to insulate the ground beneath the floor—had he stuffed it with moss?—so that, unlike any place I'd ever lived, you could walk around barefoot, naked even, and never feel so much as gooseflesh.

Unlike other drunks I've known, C. didn't snore. Our sleep was only ever interrupted by the sound of branches breaking beneath the weight of snow. I rarely heard wolves, never heard or saw a bear although I knew they were out there, saw their prints and scat. Tonight, I know they are out there. I have set booby traps and signals to wake me. I haven't forgotten the danger.

THOSE SHORT DAYS LAST fall and winter I split wood and stacked it neatly on every porch. I carted supplies to and from town, shoveled snow, patched clothes, and spent long days listening to C. read or reading aloud to him from all the many books he had collected over the years.

I had thought it a possibility, us getting together, my instincts well-honed from years in Portland. C.'s salty language, the way he stared at me before falling asleep in his chair those first few nights. I really wasn't expecting it, but was prepared to wake up from my cot, as I did the seventh morning, with C. seated beside me, soberly brushing the hair out of my eyes.

If he could tell that I was stirring awake, my inhales deeper in those brief moments before opening my eyes, he never stuttered in his rhythm running the tips of his fingers through my brown, disheveled locks. And in turn I knew that he would not flinch when I smiled, opening my eyes slowly, pivoting from laying on my side to my back, grabbing his warm hand at my cheek and moving it to my chest, letting him hear the quickening of my heart. I laugh at the romanticism of it, like a tawdry novel, the way these simple gestures echoed those of the star-crossed lovers and maudlin protagonists in books we filled our nights with.

It's a curse, this sentimentality. I must remember it as I steel myself to keep knocking on doors until I learn where C. is, or was, or if he is part and parcel of the very ash beneath me. I remember the way he kissed every part of my face, the way his tongue sometimes tasted of the sprigs of mint he chewed to mask the gin. I could remember the thrill of feeling his naked body against mine, not only when we were sweaty with sex but long after, when we slept together against the fire. I remember all the ways in which the jigsaw piece of him seemed to perfectly match the jigsaw piece of me. We laughed a lot together, with or without drink. His stories of Crawfordsville and mine of Iowa City had so many layers of overlap, we began to match the same symmetry of that cabin. Only that fractured wrist of his felt out of sync. He could do everything else—take my cock in his mouth, bury himself deep inside me—and keep returning to the well. Kiss me boldly when we were in a playful mood, which was often. Which was every day. Which was constant.

It will start snowing soon.

"No fall except the fall from grace," he'd said one night, unprompted. He lifted his healing but still hobbled arm. "This here's a reminder of Portland, of a little house with a nice attic and a little basement a few clicks east of the river, of a piano window I'd put in for her, my wife with gloriously thick, curly red hair, for the upright piano she taught lessons on. A reminder of M., our little boy with freckles and a flat, inquisitive face, always watching me, always watching the road outside. Like my flat, inquisitive face, watching you watching me now, wondering how much this wound would smart if you touched it."

It had not been a fight with his wife. The gist of it was that C. had not been particularly careful about the men he let come by to visit him in that clean basement with the door that latched and locked. It was ostensibly for liquor and cards, but the sounds that drifted up through the brick furnace were more than poker.

And G., his wife, had sized them up by their guilty faces—tender and wide-eyed—as the young men popped out of the basement again, grabbing their coat and startled into giggles at the family eating dinner by the stove, the domesticity of it all.

No, it was no fight with her, but with one of these young men, a wild one who couldn't hold his liquor and was excited and angry and scared all at once, pulled forward into pleasure only from little bites at his neck, C.'s scratches at his back, and a deep transitory calm the instant he ejaculated inside C.'s waiting body. Then a quick shift as he pulled out. Then stomach fluttering and jaw clenching, disorientation and shame welling up inside him, grabbing for C.'s clean shirt to wipe himself.

After he told me this, C.'s face shifted just as the young man's face must have shifted, repeating his words: "You are sick. This is a sickness. This is a spell you have me under. What did you do to me?"

The young man had become a stag, bucking in his basement, ripping at C.'s clothes with his antlers as he tried to put them back on. Grabbing for his belt to choke C. but lacking the nerve. Then fleeing with C. close behind, hoping to prevent what words would come out upstairs.

"I lost my balance. He pushed me back, two of us at the top of the basement stairs. One wrist caught the railing, but awkwardly and I lost my grip. I fell in a heap with my wrist crunching beneath me."

C. left Portland quickly after that. He had money stashed away, an exit plan all along, for when the time was right, or necessary.

C. laughed at himself. "I saved up for when the right man would come along," he said.

A veterinarian reset his wrist. A clerk in a lawyer's office helped drum up the right papers for a divorce. It was all so fast. He had only been established in that Lacomb cabin— what?—six weeks before I'd arrived?

AFTER WINTER, ESPECIALLY AFTER the census taker, something was lost between us. The newness had worn off. There were no more caresses when we had sex. I was still greedy about his body, but he began to take mine for granted. He drank more. And as I'd feared, I began to disappear into the symmetry, like so many framed portraits on C's mantel. Like so many sharp objects that could hurt us if we weren't careful.

He seemed to recognize this, too. And with his wrist healed, he started on a project which brought out the skills his infirmity had kept hidden. He fashioned two bracelets out of a thin piece of silver, hammering them out, using the kiln and the anvil to shape them just so. One link for his wrist and one for mine. This was not a marriage, the gift seemed to say when he presented it to me, angling the gap so it fit over my wrist, placing mine on me and having me put his on. This was not a new ritual. But it was something, a gift that brought him joy as well as pain when he saw how perfectly they matched, how perfectly they fit.

December 15, 1930

The going is slow, but steady. On my way out of Lacomb, I could have asked after C. at the general store, or at Jane's. Except I worried that if folks recognized me, and if C. were indeed dead from that fire, maybe I was the one to pin it on. Maybe they were already tracking me.

Before I left, I sifted the ashes and property for bones, or teeth, or that silver bracelet, but I couldn't find them. My own bracelet was stolen from me by one of the men I was with above A.'s camera shop. Perhaps it is shimmering on some woman's wrist right now as she washes the dishes, the only bright thing in a dark marriage.

C. is gone. Dead. I don't know how I know but I know.

I could go back to Portland, but the city's technology, its buildings and railroads and electricity, feel lost to me now.

I know the going will be hard, but I want only wilderness ahead of me, a primal reckoning.

January 1, 1931

Turns out there are sawmills and buck work in every hill and valley. Enough for a meal, a cot, but not enough to stop moving. A world propped up by dead wood.

I dreamt of the census taker last night. The year was 1940. I was living in a town on the Oregon coast. Pacific City or Cannon Beach, some place with those tremendous haystack rocks on the horizon just beyond the shore, jutting out like breaching whales. I've only seen them from pictures, but everything felt so familiar and alive in that dream, as though I'd grown up with the sea brine smell of it all.

When I answered the door, the census taker had recognized me.

"A repeat customer," she said, her eyes twinkly.

The census taker brought another woman with her to split up the work which was, she explained, tedious, block after block after block. The woman was taller than the census taker, with blond hair cut as short as a man's.

I let them in. Into a home I somehow knew I built with C. It was well-appointed and had a cliff's edge view of the haystack rock and the wide ocean expanse, shimmering with violet tones in the early evening light. But C. was somewhere else. Still napping, perhaps, or running an errand.

The census taker introduced me to her cohort.

"L—— T——," she said, addressing me by my full name. "This is K., my pardner." She drew the word out with a wink, so that I knew there was no business connotation to it. And, as if to land the point completely, the census taker took K.'s chin in her hand and drew her face to hers for a kiss. They smiled long and lovingly at each other.

I hung their coats up. I made tea.

The census taker kept looking over my shoulder, as though waiting for C. to appear.

"There are so many more of us now," the census taker said. "And more every day. We keep records. That is, we keep a separate record. It's not a question yet on the census, but K. and I are good at reading between the lines. Are you ready? Shall we get started?"

I woke after that.

As I write this, there is a mourning dove. A rain dove Mama called it. Or was it turtle dove? I know these names, but not if it's a good sign or an omen. But this is the last page of this little book I have and that seems sign enough.

Here ends the enumeration of L.P.T.

I'll leave you here, discarding the danger embedded in these pages.

I'll bury you with my memory of C., in the wild, as a wish for the decades to come, a magnet for a missing bracelet, like a compass that only points west, to the sea. A blessing for all the patchwork people looking for the train to slow down long enough they can hop on.

DOS HERMANOS

Victor

The thick, heavy doors of Dos Hermanos were the thing when we were boys, straining our triceps as we worked the golden handles together in our excitement. Back when Julien and I were a team. That glorious rush of smells— grilled onions and charred steak—as our eyes adjusted to the red leather dark lit with nothing but votives and dangly Christmas lights. We were squirts. Bolo ties and the brown pleather jackets abuela got us for Christmas. Our necks were supple, pliant in the palms of our parents, guided from the lobby to the high-backed booths in back where we'd laugh and sip Roy Rogers, house the chips, steal burps in the bathroom, and fill our bellies to bursting. One Friday a month when all of us were civil and no one fought. Then again for our birthday each November, when we got the full mariachi treatment, Julien and I not yet resentful about everything we had to share.

Now you walk in and it's just a big light-up display of shirts and hats for sale. Cheesy. You have to put your name in and wait forever. On the counter are tourist brochures—the Farmer's Market, Olvera Street, Disneyland—and those same wrapped peppermints and toothpick dispensers you find everywhere, none of the chocolate nougat stuff they used to give you. No beautiful hostess, either, standing in her beveled skirt of tulle—green and red and white—cleavage like the Grand Canyon. Only a boring dude in a dark red suit gathering menus with a yawn.

Jupes and I hang at the far end of the bar to wait for Julien. The energy is off tonight. Something in the air. Maybe the rain and the fact the patio's closed. Everyone's crammed inside with that earthy petrichor smell, and something else, something moldy tickling your nostrils. People hover and wait for tables, too cheap to buy a drink. They're on their cell phones. They're watching the playoffs. Looking around, I know pop would have already split. One step in Dos Hermanos this crowded and we would be home. Mom would order us Chinese.

"He started sending them again," Jupes says, clearing her throat to get it out twice above the din of the bar, placing the screen of her phone to face me. On it are five rows of cartoon hand emojis, like a line of high fives waiting to be slapped. Then Jupes scrolls down to a picture of a blown-out, flash-lit penis on a tiled counter. The thing is half-erect, slightly crooked and bulged at the center. An ugly dick.

"That's nasty," I say.

"I take screenshots like this, see, and just forward them to the lawyers. Like that. Done. God, imagine that was your job."

"They're paid enough to look at that. For what they got you in the divorce, they should frame that one."

"I just can't understand it. I mean, Tuck's with him right now. If I wanted to, I could call someone and get him on the first flight back to Phoenix."

"We're not in Phoenix, babe."

"I know. But if I had to, I could fly back and get him."

"Screw that. Fly Tuck out here and we go sightseeing when this wedding shit is done. What do you say?"

"Is your brother okay?"

"I don't know. Kinda high strung, no? Like he's on his period?"

You shouldn't say that she says with her eyes, her pout, but she is laughing just the same. We slide the chips and salsa closer to us. Thin, fresh chips hot and glistening with oil in their basket. Black salsa in its little stone tripod. It tastes the same as when we were kids. At least there is that.

Jupes scoots her stool closer and I move in to hug her into me. This is our sweet spot. Jupes and her round hazel eyes and her small, crooked nose. A salty kiss, lips hot from the chips, tongues cold from the margaritas. "What is it you were showing me on the TV?" she asks and our eyes drift up to the game.

"Replay is over," I say. "Nice pass is all. You want another one?" I say, pointing to her empty glass.

"Yeah, but we probably shouldn't," she says running her finger along the rim to pick up the salt she's missed. "We'll be passed out on the drive."

"Jules isn't off until ten. We'll pace ourselves."

"You love your nicknames. Jules and Jupes. We should start a podcast."

"He likes you."

"I know," she says, then flags down the bartender for menus. "I'm starving. I need meat." She spins playfully on her stool and hops off. I watch her straighten her dress a little and then I pinch her ass.

"So predictable," she says.

I pull her into me and don't let her leave. I give her three more quick kisses. When she walks away, then my heart starts to race, a lightheaded feeling as my blood drains. I'm untethered, but only for a little while.

Mom will hate her. Another gringo like our no-good father. Her dyed black hair and earnest expressiveness, the tattoos on her arms, her curves, the tight blue dress she wears when she wants them noticed. Even her name—Jupiter—and of course the fact that she's divorced like me. Julien told me Mom is still pissed she wasn't invited to our wedding, thought Jupes must be knocked up for us to do it so quickly. Except I can't have kids, remember? Mom refuses to remember these things. Or she remembers but thinks the laws of science don't belong to our family, that she has the cure for everything if I would just listen, pray, and take the goddamn supplements she ships me. I don't even want kids, but I can't say that to her.

"What do you mean it was just them and you?" she said to Julien, confused there was no priest, no church, no witnesses but Julien and Jupiter's best friend Ryan. Julien telling me all this, how he had to explain to Mom how he got ordained online and drove out. Mom telling him he was full of shit and hanging up, still hot, still pissed. That was New Year's Eve, not even six months ago.

Is this her revenge on us, Mom's wedding now? Is she going through the change? Oh, I'm saving that one up. I haven't said that to her. But that's the thing, no? She wants to make Julien and I watch her being married off, make her think she is still young and still got it. That's what she wants. Two of us sitting there, wallowing in it from the first row, her two boys that look just like their cheating, puto father (god rest his soul). We are ungrateful, clearly. We will not love her the way this flaco sailor does. God, the pictures she posts on Facebook. Ugly love, I told Jupes when I first saw him. Ugly fucking crazy fucking love. I don't even know what's in it for him. Mom has no money. The kid's an ensign. Is that what it is? Whatever you call the enlisted guy in the Navy with only one stripe on his sleeve? How did they even meet? A bar? Church? He is younger than us for fuck's sake.

The bartender delivers menus and I ask for another round of margaritas. He looks at me a little too long, curiously, as he clears and wipes the counter. He clearly knows Julien so it's the twin thing throwing him off. He is Julien's type, although I can't really say I know how I know this. Lean, but no real muscles to speak of. A yoga body with geeky glasses. Tatted up arms, sides of his head shaved high and tight with a little faux hawk that makes him look even taller. But that hipster mustache. God help me.

Jupes is not back from the bathroom but her phone is here and vibrates loudly on the bar, lighting up. I catch the bartender's eyes first, looking down at her phone, and then I get a brief glance at the picture before the phone goes dark. I know immediately what I've seen and what the bartender has seen, another picture of that stupid misshapen cock, those hairy fucking knuckles of her ex-husband's neanderthal hand choking it at the base. I turn the phone over like it's a hot coal.

The bartender moves instantly away, pretending he didn't see, leaning into another customer for an order. When he passes by again, there seems to be something he is about to say and I want to reach over and rip his mustache right off him. But I don't go there.

I look toward the lobby, in the direction of the parking lot, willing Julien to please get off early tonight.

Julien

This was our spot as kids. It's a weird feeling me working here tonight and Victor on the other side of that wall with his wife. There are so many other hustles, he said the other night. If you need money for your film, ask. It's embarrassing.

There are no windows on this side, but it's like we watch each other in our own way. Not quite telepathy but something close to it, the twin magic Mom made us believe in. He sees me jockeying back and forth in my uniform. Thinks I'm an idiot for getting a job here. He watches me hustle and say thank you and nod and take tips. He sees me being bossed around, rolls his eyes when Rudy takes the nicer cars. Maybe he hears Rudy call me maricón behind my back. He'd stick up for me, kick Rudy's ass, but he might just as easily pretend he didn't hear.

I see Victor in my own way, too, the way he chokes the neck of the margarita goblet and downs it too quickly, probably on his second already. He's also eating chips too quickly, as though he won't get anything else to eat tonight. The raw onions in the salsa always give him a stomachache and he'll need about three quality, restaurant bathrooms—no rest areas—on the drive down to San Diego. So predictable.

I see Ben waiting on him at the bar, seeing the me in Victor and curious about the Victor in me. Hair with the same no-fuss part, clean shaven, no tats. I haven't told my brother about Ben exactly. He'll be happy, I guess, in his way. He sort of shuts up about it, which is ok, and we'll have our own room at the hotel, so all is well. Jupiter figured it out. She knows Ben is coming with. We were texting about it. She knows why they are eating at the bar and not in the restaurant, that we're both getting off at ten on the dot.

I stand with Mateo under the awning because it has started to rain. Mateo has a zip-up rain hoodie and I don't. There is a client standing with us, talking on his phone as he waits for his car, but Mateo talks to me in front of him. He doesn't care. Mateo says June gloom. He says it was on the weather channel this morning. Why don't I watch the weather channel? I say that I grew up here. The whole point is not to watch the weather channel. Just look out the window.

The other valets are all talking about the game, giving updates. Someone's got it streaming on their phone. Since when does everyone care about the Clippers? Victor will be watching this game, too. He can't get into the Suns, still misses the Lakers in their heyday. I see him pinching Jupiter's ass. I really do like her a lot. She's good at giving him shit, but in the right way. I love her hippie name: Jupiter. And I love the pull of the big planet, the wise sage in her chart. She is already more warm and down to earth than the last one. Victor calls her Jupes. I like that, too. I can tell that Phoenix has been good for them. He's there at the bar and he is feeling that he has a better job now. He's back where he came from and his beautiful new wife is with him and things are good. Who cares that Mom's getting married to some flaco sailor with a shaved, misshapen head and acne scars?

SOMETIMES YOU CAN HEAR the clunky cars coming down Pico and slowing down and know they are about to turn in here. You just know. Mateo and I look at each other because we hear one of these and then we watch this enormous white van, dented and dirty, as it coughs and wheezes, turning slowly into the lot. Mateo and I try and direct it closer to the awning, so the guests can stay dry the whole way up the ramp and into the restaurant, but the woman driving pulls in at an odd angle, a good ten feet from the awning which throws everything off. Rudy has just driven up with the Benz of the guy on the phone waiting and Rudy could back up, let the guy get in at the curb, but there's already someone else behind him; he's boxed in. Now it's a giant cluster where everyone's going to have to wait until the van is gone. Phone guy sees it all go down and I can tell he's already slipping his tip back in his pocket. Rudy will yell at us for sure and if another car comes in soon after the van, everything's going to blow up.

My brother can see all this go down. Somehow, through that wall. He's rolling his eyes again at the shit I'm willing to put up with for some extra weekend cash.

This stupid van.

A giant exits the passenger side. Super white. Basement hermit white, with water beading strangely down his scalp and forehead, like he's got on special lotion or makeup. The giant pulls at the side door until it slides open to reveal a robotic wheelchair ramp whirring and beeping as it slowly unfurls. As the giant waits, his whole body seems to squint to seek shelter from the drizzle. His scalp is a shiny bulb of white moving against the backdrop of storm clouds in the distance. I truly can't tell if his Hawaiian shirt and cargo shorts are sticking to him because of the rain or the tang of sweat I smell in the air. I help secure the ramp in place. I can just make out other faces from the hot commotion inside the minivan. They are waiting as we are waiting. At least three cars, maybe more, backed up on Pico are waiting. The dude with the Benz is waiting along with another couple that have just left the restaurant. The ugly white van itself is waiting, clicking and wheezing, chiming from the key still in the ignition.

Mateo holds a maroon golf umbrella over the old woman in the wheelchair that slides out. She is dressed in a flower-print muumuu and sandals, a red do-rag on her head, like abuela after rounds of chemo. Her flabby forearms grip the armrests as she is wheeled down. She wears no makeup, no jewelry, and her toenails are grey and long and chipped at the edges. She looks sedated, resigned to her fate, as though she has no idea where she is, as though they have kidnapped her from the assisted living place and told her nothing.

The giant gets his mother rolled under the awning and out of the way, then abandons her as he trots up to the restaurant alone. Get their name on the list, I suppose. Meanwhile, the van exhales six more people: five tall teenage boys and the driver, the giant's wife, a skeletal woman whose body looks shrunken inside her sweatpants and Mickey Mouse sweatshirt. Road-hard, Victor would call her, with her poofed out Aileen Wuornos hair. She doesn't even look directly at me, simply hands me the keys and takes my ticket. She herds her pack and prompts her oldest to roll his grandmother up the ramp to the restaurant.

As I drive the van away, I crank the window open to clear out the dust and damp. I can feel everyone's eyes on me. Mateo at the kiosk of keys, and Rudy getting out of the Benz in my rearview. Even Victor and Jupiter inside the restaurant and the family from the van. Someone yells out and I brake, suddenly, thinking they're shouting at me, maybe to tell me a door is open or the lights need to go on. But in the side-view mirror I see it's just the crew with their phones out, streaming the game and pointing to some play. It's not about me at all.

Victor

Jupes returns to the bar and I point to her phone on the table.

"Her ex-husband's a whack job," I shout to the bartender, who is too far away to hear what I'm saying. Everyone is yelling because the Clippers just landed a three to tie the game in the final fraction of a second. They'd been on a 15-0 run. Somehow this still pisses me off, too. Since when are we all rooting for the Clippers?

"Did you two want to order food?" the bartender asks, returning with our second round.

"Yes," I say. I look over at Jupiter who is forwarding the next picture to the lawyers. I order for us and Jupes gives a thumbs up. I ask the bartender about closing time, about Julien, but he acts sort of strange and keeps looking over at Jupes instead of me.

She smiles way too politely at him, breathing him in. "You're Ben, right?"

He nods.

"Obviously this is Julien's brother, Victor. I'm Jupiter, his wife."

I notice Ben's rings when we shake his hand, turquoise and onyx in carved silver bands. Gorgeous work.

"Of course. I didn't want to say until—I mean—it's nice to meet you both."

"Where'd you get those, man? Your rings?"

Someone at the other end of the bar yells something.

"One sec, sorry," Ben says and excuses himself.

"What just happened?" I say, confused.

"That's Julien's boyfriend, you idiot. Why do you think

he keeps staring at you?"

"What? How do you know that?"

"Julien texted me. We text."

I finish my last margarita in one brain-freezey gulp and start in on the second.

"Watch that. Your brother shouldn't have to drive the whole way after he's been working. That's your last one."

"He said he wants to drive!"

"I'm just saying. He probably just wants to chill," Jupes says in the direction of the bartender, not to me.

"His name is Ben?"

"Don't give him a hard time, he's just doing his job."

"You know they used to bring margaritas to the table on fire. They'd have this little boat made from lime peel that sat on top of the drink, with just enough alcohol they could light it up. They don't have style anymore."

But Jupes isn't listening. Now she's staring toward the TV, not really watching. Ruminating about something. Then she watches my brother's boyfriend again, the way he concentrates on making the drinks on his list. I watch her sip her drink and I sip mine. She looks over at me and smiles and leans her head into my shoulder for a second.

Where is a good embarrassing picture of Julien so I can show it to Ben, make sure he knows what I'm talking about, what it was like coming here to Dos Hermanos when it felt old-school. How I made fun of Julien when he told me he was working here. Shouldn't you be on a set or something, learning the craft? Why do you have to be someone's valet, smile for shit tips? No wonder he didn't listen. Stubborn as me. And I probably sounded like Mom. Julien said this was close to his apartment and rent was rent and when I asked him about taking more film classes, about his writing, he dodged and changed the subject.

Jupiter's head is back on my shoulder. Our stomachs grumble in sync. I can see her little features in the barback mirror. The nose, the eyes, those beautiful lashes she doesn't have to embellish at all with anything. She's tanned so much in Phoenix, she's darker than me.

"Ben saw that picture pop up on your phone," I say.

"No! What did you say?"

"I think he thought it was for me. I told him I just have a slutty wife."

"No you didn't, asshole! Did he really see it? That's embarrassing."

"For your ex maybe, not for you. Why do you let that jerk get to you like that?"

She sips some water which makes her hiccup and she begins to laugh again. "He's cute, you know. Ben. That little mustache. I can see him and Julien together."

"Really? We're doing that now? You want me to see what time he gets off? Maybe he can come with us to the wedding."

"He *is* coming, Victor. With all of *us*. To San *Diego*. Mind like an iron trap you have."

"Can we not have this discussion now?"

"God, you're in a mood. Watch your stupid game."

And like that, I look up and realize the game's over. The Clippers lost.

Julien

We still have a few compact spots left but nothing that will fit the van. I have to park it on the street. But I can't keep it here. I'll have to hustle back to move it or we get called in by neighbors and could get a ticket, or worse: a tow. Nightmare all night.

I'm standing in front, jotting the license plate and the name of the cross-street on the back of the ticket in case someone else has to get it. You can see it from the back lot, can't miss it really, but you want to be sure. At least they have a disabled placard. That might help.

I'm about to close the door, making sure I have the key and everything when, fuck all to hell, a huge dog lumbers forward out of nowhere, panting and staring at me from the driver's seat. Is this magic, a conjuring of some kind? Where did it come from? And why didn't I hear it at all from inside the van? I try and close the door on it, but it is too heavy and it knocks me into the street as it climbs out. Big and stocky like a rottweiler, with eyes wide apart like a pit and short fur the color of cappuccino. It looks back at me panting, the halo glow of the streetlamp reflecting off its tongue. It is laughing at me, then hobbles away with a strange goofy gait down the street.

"Hey!" I yell, as though it will respond, which it doesn't. It stops and sniffs the wheel of a car. I am up and running toward it now, but it jaunts ahead of me again before I can get it.

When we were little, my brother and I both wanted a dog but Mom said no. A thousand times no. She said she was allergic and not until we were older did we realize this was a lie. She simply hated dogs. Crossed the street to avoid them. And she was so rude about it, too. Told us all dogs were monsters, like toddlers at first, shitting and pissing everywhere. They hurt you or run away, they make you sad. Los duendes she called them. The goblins. Little devils.

After pop left, we asked for a dog to protect us—a good duende, a helpful duende—but she refused. Told us horror stories instead. Pit bull duendes that ate children's faces. German shepherd duendes that disemboweled their owners. She'd even find us gruesome pictures to prove her point. When a neighbor's poodle went in heat and was kept in a cage lined with newspaper, with blood matted all over her white fur, mom stayed outside and forced us to go in to look at the mess. When one of my friend's mom had us over for dinner and mom caught her male dachshund screwing the teddy bear I had brought for sleepover, she looked at me, saying with her eyes what she wouldn't say aloud in front of company, that that little bouncy thing with its bright red erection, that there foreshadowed death and destruction, see, I told you.

The rottweiler duende from the van moves faster than it looks like it should, its awkward gallop through the puddles of rain favoring one side so that her midsection is bowed, like she will go around in circles instead of straight. But this doesn't matter. She is on a good run now, indifferent to cross traffic, block by block in the quiet residential streets that run parallel to Pico. She only stops so that she can take a shit, and this is the only way I catch her, in that vulnerable way she looks up at me, a stranger, as she relieves herself in one large, nose-curdling pile.

An old man smoking a cigarette in the entryway of an apartment complex watches me as I hug the duende, fingers underneath the collar and another arm around its wide flank as it finishes. All the while it has begun to rain harder. I am soaked through already and the dog is wet and trying to shake the wet off, so it's a struggle keeping my grip. My sweat mixed with the dog's wet fur makes my eyes water.

The man from the apartment glares at me as I pull the duende away. His eyes are saying he doesn't want to get wet but that under other circumstances he would confront me, call someone if I don't clean up that shit. I don't care if he believes me or if he can see my uniform in the dark. It takes all my concentration and power to get this dog to follow me, not sniff anything, and to get back to the van. I can feel my phone vibrating in my pocket, but I can't answer it without letting go of the duende.

Victor

I want to tell someone: screw this restaurant. I want to tell someone: it's so sad how you've gone commercial, how you're so branded now, turned into a caricature of a Mexican restaurant instead of the real deal. I want to say fuck you to the rain-soaked crowd I have to fight to get to the bathroom, this lobby full of tourists and wheelchairs and stupid gangly teenagers who don't even dress up for dinner. Fuck the tile bathroom and all the automatic everything in there. No more little piles of nice towels. No chiclet gum. No orange potpourri in a crystal bowl. It used to be as dark as the restaurant in here, maybe a few candles going. Not now. It's all bright and flat, like they had to bring it up to some lousy city code.

And that funky smell from the bar and lobby, it's here, too. Faulty pipes, soaked mats, some cheap cleaning product, I don't know. How I hate these hot cities when it rains because it reminds you of how dirty the place must be the rest of the time.

And this tourist here. This giant, soaking wet in his shorts and a Hawaiian shirt, his hairy feet in flip-flops, skin whiter than the urinal. A freak of nature. His sweat or the last guy's sweat sharp on the nose in the hotbox of that bathroom.

"Are they all still out there!?" the giant whisper-yells at me as I brace myself in the corner to pee.

"What are you talking about, guy?"

"My family. Did you see them? Old lady in a wheelchair, some tall teenagers, short mousy woman."

"I guess," I say.

"I need to get out of here," the man says.

"Deep breaths, Kemosabe. Shit's fine. You're fine. I'm going to pee and then I'll be fine."

I'm at the urinal but looking over my shoulder at the giant, who is looking at himself in the mirror, blubbering, his white face now a bag of red peppers. Why does anyone marry anyone? Why does anyone hitch themselves on to other people's crazy? This poor lump here in the bathroom? The pathetic ass my Mom's about to marry. Can that sailor's name really be Jesús? Do Julien and I really have to compete with that?

I wash my hands as quickly as I can but they have those stupid old drying machines that take forever. The giant is watching me through the mirror's reflection.

"Tell me that again," he blurts over the whir of the machine. "Tell me I'm fine. Call me Kemosabe. Tell me everything's going to be okay."

"Shit's on you," I say, but before I can get the hell out of there, he grabs my shoulder.

"Please, friend. Just one thing. Please. Tell me if they're still out there in the lobby or if they've been seated. Tell me that one thing. Please."

I need to get out of there, and maybe it's the margaritas that have made me so gracious, so willing to do what this poor pathetic man has asked me to. I give him a wink. I got you Kemosabe, you crazy albino Kemosabe. I leave the restroom and check the lobby. The giant's family isn't there. So I pop back in and say the coast is clear and don't really hear what he says after that, but I think it's "thank you," or more likely, "thank God."

I go the long way around the restaurant, check out everyone eating and talking and drinking and laughing, to get all the way back to the bar the other way, bypassing the crowded lobby. For a brief instant, I see the giant's family in a corner by the fireplace, a spot where they can get the grandma's wheelchair in. But I don't stop or linger. I'm smiling the whole time, giggling almost, because of this radio program that used to play in our house, something on AM that Mom used to listen to, the only thing she liked to listen to in English. *EGBOK in the Morning* was their catchphrase, the hollow piece of meat they threw out every day to people like Mom whose faith in things was as eclectic as her taste in men, who picked up any thread of inspirational mumbo-jumbo she found in the moment, who ate that shit up. *EGBOK in the Morning. EGBOK, EGBOK!* they clucked like chickens. It stood for Everything's Gonna

Be OK. Egbok. Now I send that cheesy egbok vibe to the albino in the bathroom, wherever he's off to now, and then I send it to Julien. Jupes is smiling when I come back and, before I say anything, I send egbok vibes to her, too.

Julien

I am so focused on where the duende needs to be, back in its van, and how the van needs to be in the other lot, the self-park one, that I completely lose track of where I am, on Pico now but blocks away from Dos Hermanos. The rain has turned into a monsoon, sideways and heavy. Victor inside there, through the wall, somehow sensing all of this, wanting nothing more than to leave right now so we can get started on whatever Mom has planned for us in San Diego. Victor, wanting nothing more than to say to me I told you so. Don't go working in a dump like this, it's beneath you. And Ben works here so he is beneath me, too, I suppose, even though it's Ben that sort of has his shit together. A dog, plants, a savings account. I essentially live with him now.

We squat beneath an awning, the duende and I. We're friends now. She licks rain off my face, my nose, my hair. An army of licks, her breath warm and fishy. Her collar has no information. No number to call, no name. All dogs are dirty boys, Mom says, but this duende is a sweet, plus-sized girl with a rebellious heart. She has no shame, no agenda.

123

Victor's rented Escalade is in the lot right there. Why not? I've got his keys. What if I open it up and lift the duende into the back? She'd be heavy, but maybe being cradled like that, she'd turn as pliant and listless as if I'd tranquilized her. We could adopt her, Victor or Ben and I, pretending at first that she is the wedding gift for mom and Jesús. Oh my god, that makes me laugh.

The duende is excited about this possibility, too. She stands up, then sits down gingerly, sideways, favoring one side like one leg is hurt or arthritic, but not for long before she bolts up again. Excited or maybe excited and scared, I can't tell. There is the beginning of a growl, a rumbling in her gut on its way to a bark.

Then I hear it, a sound coming toward us from the west along Pico. The same rattle and whine, the same brake hiss of that stupid van. It can't be of course. I have the keys. But following her growls and watching it come toward us, there is no mistaking it. The dented driver's side door. The headlights with strange casings that make them look like black eyes. It picks up steam as it heads our way, squealing and groaning and revving until it soars right past us. The giant is behind the wheel, looking over just long enough to lock eyes with me standing with his dog, his duende now barking gloriously for him, drooling, wagging her tail, shaking so hard I can barely keep hold of her.

The look is brief but I can tell his eyes are bloodshot because there is no more white left in them. He looks forward again, gunning the engine and speeding to the wide intersection, where he makes an impossibly fast turn onto Western, barely missing another car honking at it, skidding to catch itself. I expect to hear a crash, but there isn't one. The sound of the van fades and dies and disappears forever into the wall of rain.

Perhaps this is fate. Perhaps Victor and I will steal the duende away so it's not part of that mess anymore. We won't give it to mom because she'd never take it and, besides, the joke would only last so long. But we'll give her a good home. Either with Ben and I, when we make it official, or I sneak her into my own apartment for a while and hope she doesn't bark, hiding her as long as I can before we drive her out to Phoenix to live with Victor. He's got so much more room.

The traffic is light now. I've lost all track of time and it's not until there's a lull in the rain that I truly feel how soaking wet I am.

Then I hear it again, the van coming back around, only slower this time, idling to a stop on the far side of the road an ocean of wet asphalt away. The van snaps and crackles like a campfire, waiting. And before I realize what is happening, the duende breaks free of my grip to run straight for it. It is a long shot. Jesus. Whether by sixth sense or not, the girl gets lucky. Pico is all stopped at lights and by the time she reaches the intersection, the other side is stopped and she makes it all the way to the passenger side of the van, a door the giant has leaned over to open for her. She lumbers up easily, moving behind him to the warm belly of the van until their getaway is complete.

Victor and Julien

Do we know already that it will be us, a *we* again? Not the whole drive to San Diego, but most of it? If not on our lips, then in the air-conditioned bliss of that ride, the tricked-out Escalade we rented? Our lives crossing paths again, as even divergent storylines inevitably do, snapping back into place to head in the same direction. Little squirts again in our bolo ties and pleather jackets. Things we can't put in words because, after all that telepathy, we're still developing a language.

Some of the ride we'll be mute, side by side in front. Jupes in back making conversation with Ben. The duende we'll pretend is there, quiet and sleeping soundly in the way way back, a gag gift for mom but really a new thing for all of us to tend to.

Jupes and Ben will tease out everything until our stories roll together. About Dos Hermanos. Pop ordering for us, Mom disagreeing with everything. Drinking Shirley Temples, which we still called Roy Rogers even though it had ginger ale. Housing the chips. Holding onto burps until we got to that dark little bathroom with the orange potpourri. Mom and her hatred of dogs.

And that other story that hangs over everything, that we'll keep thinking about the rest of the way, the dark myths that binds us again: about giants who leave their villages to abscond with the devil.

THE DELAWARE GAP

The fill-in for Dr. Cohen swabbed a heavy salve on my neck, shoulders, and arms, humming to himself as he massaged my skin the way a privileged prince might were he delighted in a recent art acquisition or presiding over the funeral of someone disagreeable. His bony fingers probed each set of muscles as he asked if I'd ever been badly burned there. My pores obeyed, absorbing his cold medicine and finding the ancient heat embedded within them.

I told this prince, Dr. Singh, the same story I'd told Dr. Cohen, about the record heat at the Delaware Gap years ago, the college trip inner-tubing the river, and how like an idiot I used hand lotion instead of anything with SPF.

"There's always someone has it worse," I said, retelling a story about a former track star who'd launched himself from a trail high up the Pennsy side of the Gap and died that same summer. "They said he'd been disoriented on account of sun poisoning and drugs in his system."

"That's a shame," he said. He placed his glasses on before leaning in and numbing my skin in two other spots he had circled with red marker, one at the base of my neck, the other on my right thigh, just above the knee.

"Friends he was hiking with said he jumped off the cliff thinking wings were going to take him," I added, turning my head away from the sharp tools in the doctor's delicate hands. It took only seconds for him to cut his scoops from me, two little tugs. It felt like nothing at all. Then more salve, some band-aids, and that was it.

"Done," he said, ripping his latex gloves off and gesturing with them to my piles of clothes.

"He landed on the branch of a tree whose seed must have sprouted thirty, forty years before he was born, its arm held out in just the right way to make the catch. There's something to that, isn't there?"

The doctor nodded and removed his glasses. "Perhaps," he offered and then said, as he closed the door slowly behind him, "You can put your clothes back on and settle up with the receptionist. She'll give you a number to call tomorrow."

Tomorrow was Saturday, but maybe you could call on the weekend. I didn't ask. Maybe Cohen's lab ran this stuff day and night. Maybe everyone in New York had what I had, our tiny scoops of skin racked on trays lined with wax paper in storage somewhere, room after room of biopsies, labeled by patient number, waiting.

His name was Dr. Singh, but on the long walk home I kept pronouncing it *singe*. Dr. Singe. This tickled me somewhere deep, an electric twitch in my stomach I couldn't stop if I tried.

Hannah scolded me for walking, for wasting time walking from the Lower East Side to Brooklyn. We were hours behind on laundry and packing. Hannah stood in the epicenter of the chaos, bending over Colin and stacks of clothes to kiss me. Instead of asking about my appointment, a cache of questions she'd stockpile until Colin was asleep, she simply reminded me I still had to pick up the rental car.

I took Colin with me because he looked to be drowning in the piles of closet junk in the way of our camping gear. I snatched him up from a stack of sweaters and Christmas decorations and Hannah's eyes followed us, scoring me like a loss-prevention guard who isn't allowed to follow the shoplifter, only shake her head and report to management.

The hallway outside our apartment smelled of jasmine and sandalwood, something pleasant covering up something else—the trash chute, or the last rat to be caught in the laundry room. Colin twisted in my arms and we looked at each other, scrunching our faces, until he pinched my nose tight with his little hand and that was the last straw! I put him down and made him chase me out of there.

As we walked, I quizzed him on everything, making

sure he accumulated a set of facts to pivot his day on—the genus of birds and trees, different models of cars, the pronunciation of every dish on the takeout menus hanging in windows.

The rental car place wasn't far, only a few blocks, and when Colin picked out our rental from a binder of pictures, he picked a big SUV with a roof rack we didn't need.

"Why that one?"

"Because it's red!"

"They may not have the red one, bud."

"Then we'll paint it!"

AFTERWARD, WE STOOD BY the gate the rental car place shared with an auto shop, waiting for the attendant to drive Colin's pick from the garage. Colin pointed to the columns of piled tires inside the gate, stacked taller than we could reach, even if he stood on my shoulders. I pictured lifting him up, his leaning in, my accidentally dropping him into the hole and Colin trapped in all that rubber, unable to find him again. The twitch in my stomach returned, less funny now, more of an omen. I lifted Colin back into my arms, feeling how strong and heavy he was getting.

Years ago, at the last gas station before the launch spot, Hannah and me, Tyler and Bucky and all the rest, the eight of us waited our turn at the tire pumps to inflate our thick black inner tubes. We'd already stripped to our swimsuits and old sneakers, dumped ice over canned beer in the cooler, threw sandwiches and fruit on top. Hannah at nineteen was so freckled and pale that her green eyes seemed to glow in the shadows of her face. She narrowed them in concentration as Bucky showed her how to work the nozzle. Sucking hard on her last clove cigarette, Hannah was careful to ash it away from the tire as he helped her. Bucky's cheek was so close to the narrow ledge of Hannah's clavicle, he could turn and nibble on it the way I liked to do. But he didn't. He grabbed the next tire and began filling it. Hannah tossed her finished donut in the air, her bony shoulders revealing the torqued-up strength she'd hidden there—taut tennis muscles that pushed and pulled as she squeezed the donut to test its firmness. She winked her glowing eyes back at me.

Colin moved my head to face him, breaking the daydream. His eyes were green twins of his mom's, so round they reflected the whole street behind me. He ran his hands across my beard which hurt but made him giggle.

"Am I a furry monster?"

"Nooooooo, you're Dad."

"I thought I was a monster! I thought I was supposed to eat you for lunch."

In his laughter and giddiness, Colin's feet kicked at my belly, jangling the weight I'd accumulated in the years since the Delaware. At the same time his arms tightened around my neck, and the place where Dr. Singh took his pound of flesh began to burn. Beyond Colin's head, the stack of tires loomed larger, as though something were quietly growing inside it, the real monster ready to burst forth. Colin squirmed and I dropped him, a movement so quick he must have felt like I was throwing him to the pavement. He landed squarely on his feet but I could sense he was ready to cry.

"Sorry, bud."

I wanted to say more but a silver Cherokee arrived and took Colin's attention instead. It was so big and clean and new looking, he didn't care about anything else. He wanted to start the adventure. On the short drive back with the windows down he named the color of every car we passed, rattling them off as though broadcasting it to the world.

On the Delaware, Bucky would boast of his knowledge the same way, naming the towns beyond every inlet and bend of the river, shout the make and model of old cars. He'd grown up not far from the water, in Bethlehem. Bucky knew the best sites to launch, the best shops for tubes and good beer, the routine of doubling back with a second car to set up camp, the best campsites. On day hikes, we folded quietly into his wake because he'd know the rotting planks on the footbridge you had to step over. Even when he drove, he would catalogue the constellation of cigarette burns in the dark upholstered bench of his father's Caddy, fingering them without ever taking his eyes off the road.

WHEN COLIN PRESENTED THE rental car to Hannah, her

eyes went straight to the roof rack and the three semi-deflated inner tubes tied with bungie cords there.

"Where did those come from?"

"Trade secret," I said, pulling Colin closer to me.

THE FURTHER NORTH WE GOT, the quieter the car became. We knew we had left too late, that we'd need to bother the site host after hours, for wood, and use headlamps to set up, that Colin would be cranky, and that nothing was going to feel at all right again until morning, if then.

We stopped at every rest stop. Hannah said it was all the tea she drank, but I could see her red puffy eyes whenever she labored to bend herself back into the car. This pregnancy was worse on her than when she had Colin. And this trip wasn't about us, not really. It was Colin's trip. We had promised him camping, a lake to fish on. Plans and site reservations we made in the dead of winter, before the pregnancy, before Dr. Cohen and Dr. Singh.

For weeks Colin's favorite joke was a variation on a theme: "those fish aren't going to fish themselves!" For the hour and a half it took to get out of the city that afternoon, it was "the tires are not going to tire themselves!"

When Colin went down for an unexpected nap, Hannah asked again about the doctor's visit. She spoke in whispers, not looking at my face but at my legs and my arms, the back of my neck and the small bandage there.

"I told Dr. Singh the same story I told Cohen," I said.

"About the Delaware, my epic sunburn, all the blisters after. I've got a number to call next week. No sense in writing the obituary until then."

"That's not funny. And I still can't believe Cohen cancelled."

"Did you go outside yesterday? Everyone cancelled on everyone." I swept my arms around as if taking in more than the first warm days of spring, as if taking in the whole universe. "I mean, feel it right now, it's Titty Tuesday."

Hannah's hand found mine resting on the gear.

"Don't say that. You know I hate that phrase. Bucky used to say that." Hannah freed her other hand from her thighs, smeared tears and eyeliner off her cheek with her palm.

I brought her hand up and kissed it gently. "Sorry."

"Last night, I kept thinking about my grandma Ruth," Hannah said. "She used to take me into the city on these museum field trips. Every time, waiting for the subway, her hand like a seatbelt across my chest, holding me back. 'Mind the gap,' she'd say. Mind the gap."

"Mind the gap," I repeated. "Like the Delaware Gap."

Hannah looked out the passenger window.

"You know the guy filling in for Cohen was named Singh—S-I-N-G-H—but I keep pronouncing it *singe*. That's kind of funny, right?"

"You're really striking out on the gallows humor here."

Mind the gap. Isn't that what we'd been doing these last

136

six years? Except when Bucky's name was in the air. Then it was impossible.

I'VE LET IT SLIP AND slide and morph, but Hannah sees and hears it in perfect detail without much effort. Beginning with the spray bottle in Bucky's glove box, the one his father kept for when the dogs got hot. She had watched Bucky use its mist on me after everyone else had gone to sleep, after that long lazy river day, and nearly missing the drop-off spot and having to carry the gear on the trails back to camp. I'd joined Bucky at the shore, the two of us testing whether more bourbon would make our insides feel hotter than our skin. We were both so burned. So impossibly red. Hannah had stirred awake and poked herself out of the tent, wondering where I'd gone. She tracked Bucky and I north of camp, watched Bucky and I wade into the water under that canopy of stars, spraying and refilling the bottle, two silhouettes wading up to our thighs in the slow-moving water. And then that moment between us. When Bucky pulled me close to him, and the magnets locked in place.

"How is it that two men can kiss so violently," Hannah had asked, the first time she'd confessed to seeing us, the first time we'd had the talk. How is it she could see the veins in our neck and the lines of our jaws all the way out there in the dark?

It is something I do, forgetting it was something I did, that it was something I participated in. I used to blame the delirium of the sun poisoning itself, the overload of Vitamin D that made you nauseated and so sensitive to touch, you began to disassociate, move out of yourself to feel less of the pain.

And so I see it from Hannah's point of view instead of my own, a movie playing, watching from further down the shore, the wide shot of the Delaware River shimmering in the moonglow, some underbrush blurry and out of focus in the corners of the frame. The two figures stripping free of their trunks, wading deeper until the water kissed their white cocks and red bellies, easing the pain a bit more. Watching as they are far enough out that no one can see, watching as they kiss without embracing, not wanting to feel the abrasive fire of skin to skin, at first, then slowly giving in to it, forgetting the heat in the cool lapping river. Swimming in it.

I PIVOTED THE REARVIEW to see if Colin was still asleep. His eyes were closed, but he yawned big, his mouth hinging open and closed so that for a second it was as though Hannah was throwing her voice, as though her voice was coming from his lips.

"You always say you were the only ones," Hannah-Colin said before my eyes were back on the road. "But it wasn't just you and Bucky that got burned that trip. All of us did."

WE KEPT COLIN ASLEEP in the car as we made camp. It was twilight already, the new moon hiding below the horizon, and we had to swap out the batteries in our headlamps before we could do much of anything. Hannah set to work on the tent and food and I collected kindling for the fire since the site hosts were all out. I culled from the dense forest around us, pretending at least for a few minutes we were the only souls out there, letting the sounds of other campsites fade, their laughter and crackling fires drowned by the sounds of crickets, the rustle of wind through the pines, the lake water lapping at the rocks along the shore.

Could we swim after Colin went to bed? Or would it be too cold?

"I don't want to lose you," Hannah said when I popped my head into the tent to check on her. She reached over to touch my hair, tugging it hard the way she used to when it was down to my shoulders. She kissed me the way we used to between classes. Hard and a little sloppy.

"I'm here."

Then Colin called out from the car and our tears turned to laughter.

"He's going to be such a weirdo tonight."

COLIN TOLD US HIS OWN campfire stories. No monsters, but plenty of dinosaurs and cows and whatever else he picked up from his last field trip at school, the last cartoons he watched. What a spectacular sponge.

Bucky told stories this way, where everything came alive in his hands and his eyes, where you got caught up in all of it, even the Jersey accent he never quite shook. Hannah and I weren't this way. We were the wallflowers at the party. We had a thousand inside jokes and nicknames for others, but trying to relate to anyone outside the two of us, now three? We swallowed the things we should say. So how had Colin picked up his talent, his fearlessness in shouting across the aisle of the grocery store, proclaiming his place in the world? Was it simply growing up in New York? Was it an East Coast thing? Hannah had been pregnant with Colin when we found out Bucky died. Maybe some spark of him somehow found its way to Colin? Is there even a word for that kind of transference?

After dinner and the smores, after we put the last meager branches on, I noticed it. Hannah was massaging my shoulders. She had to be staring at the bandage, imagining the pattern of the scoop Dr. Singh cut out, the results still pending on a tray in a room, results of how deeply we'd been burned. Colin's head was in the night sky, his eyes expectantly waiting the next shooting star. But straight ahead, behind him, I noticed the silver jeep reflecting the flames of our campfire, turning the car red.

"Look, bud," I said, pointing. "You got the color you wanted."

He looked at me, confused, then turned around and saw it.

"Red jeep!" he shouted so loud it echoed sharply across the lake. Even he looked a little embarrassed at how loud it had come out, looking back at us to see if it was okay or not okay.

I looked up at Hannah behind me. "Ready?" I asked and she nodded.

"Red jeep!" we shouted in unison.

HICCUP'S BLUFF

The morning before his brother's funeral, Aidan Mitchell removed from a chest of blankets at the foot of his bed two items: one bottle of Johnnie Walker Blue Label a politician once gifted their father, and a plain wooden carton of cigars his grandson brought back from Santo Domingo. He placed these items on the small table in the entryway so he wouldn't forget them when, that afternoon, he and his wife Carmela would bundle themselves up in scarves and old army coats and drive their pick-up to Jackson's Saloon over on Second. There they planned to sit and brim with the booze, telling war stories as afternoon dusked into evening, stopping only when the brisk black night wore out its welcome and they'd tumble back home.

The saloon sat firmly in the center of Canyon Crossing,

a town of three avenues and seven streets that crisscrossed each other with remedial simplicity before their limbs stretched out in all directions to farm homes, factories, and the jagged creek running slow and turbid to Palo Duro. Placing wagers with the old-timers as to which appeared first, the Mitchells or the saloon, was never advised. It was a trick question. The dual rows of brick facades along Second went up in 1842 and it was this construction, spotted across the scarred plain, that first attracted the pioneer Mitchells to canyon country. The town, its mortar, and all those bastard Mitchells hardened together.

Nowadays, Jackson's was as good and dark a place as any in town to drink whiskey and watch football, some nights fútbol. The corner flatscreens provided strobes of color, the jukebox a whiff of history and Jackson, stoic as carved boulders, tended his own bar for the likes of his favorite regulars: Jessup Farragut, Conrad McMillan, and whichever Mitchell brother decided to show. They were his best customers and hogged the smooth cherry bartop night after night like wrinkled mystics indifferent to the games and prevailing language—gargoyles protecting the church of drink.

That night Aidan had gotten such an unusually early start with Carmela that by evening the premium scotch and cheap cigars were burning exceptionally bright in his head. Carmela talked with Jackson and the other regulars while Aidan retreated into himself, quietly blinking at his ghostly figure in the barback's mirror. The image—face pocked and veiny, a grizzled beard and thinning wisps of silver atop a freckled crown—was certainly no match for the bucking bronco he once was. There was the photograph taken of him in the Spring of '64, posing with Brendan and their father on the day the rubber factory doubled its footprint and its new wing went online. Tight-fitting flannels and denim, steel-toed boots and sharp white helmets so bright the shadows never seemed to darken their strident amber faces. Only two of those photos still existed, one crammed with other mementos at the union ballroom, the other in a frame on Aidan's mantel. It was this second one that Carmela had blown up onto poster board, the one that sat patiently on the mortuary easel waiting to greet everyone at tomorrow's show.

As the hours rolled along, Aidan mumbled a few slivers of a eulogy he'd been trying to compose. It lacked anything to latch onto and he could feel the line constantly slipping. Carmela kept yapping with Jackson and the bar's younger patrons distracted him with their easy laughter and the way they chugged and jeered at the games. *Flunked and drunk and full of spunk*, Brendan would say. They all conspired to make the hiccups come again, the ones in his chest as well as the ones in Aidan's head that made all the pictures slide a little.

Normally Carmela would feel something amiss in her husband's rhythms, would recognize when these visions were coming, Aidan's eyes vibrating in search of false horizons. But she took no notice of him until at last he stood, grabbed the scotch bottle and tucked it firmly into the crook of his arm.

"Going outside," he said.

She looked at him as though he were a stranger, which often he was, then shook her head and patted his brow with the sleeve of her sweater. He squinted, trying to see the street beyond the two front windows, the tiny panes old and warped with sagging glass. He thought he saw what the whole town had been expecting: a rare dusting of October snow that would blanket Canyon Crossing and bring a sense of calm out where the atoms were slow.

"It's a lot easier when you drink from the swill, honey. We didn't need to bring our own," Carmela said, shaking her head at him.

"I'll be back."

Outside, Aidan realized that there was no snow. Another hiccup, perhaps. It was the starkness of the new lights in the Fairway parking lot that had tricked his eyes. But these imaginary glows hadn't been the only things playing tricks with Aidan's mind of late. On his long morning drives to the West Amarillo VA, Aidan had begun to see flocks of swifts, flitting in all directions like bats escaping dawn. They'd bob and dance, surrounding his car, then disappear along the endless wires as quickly as they'd appeared. Aidan called them hiccups because they were simultaneously jarring and harmless. But Aidan had begun to wonder if they forebode something else, something coming his way now that the world was down one Mitchell.

Aidan sat on a rusting iron bench, one of several along the main strip that the town voted to install but rarely maintained. He unearthed a fresh cigar from his pocket, clipped the leafed-over end with his teeth and took several short cloudy drags as he lit it. Across the street, crowding the front window of the restaurant across Second, he could make out Phil Gilchrist Sr. and his wife and their growing family—Phillip Jr. and wife, ugly Wendy and her ugly husband, and all the loud, coarse grandchildren.

"You coming?" his wife asked, appearing beside him on the bench as she pulled out her Salems and smacked her pack against her palm.

"Gilchrist on a cross is over there." Aidan closed one eye and pointed his cigar as though to singe Phil's little face in the window.

Carmela watched her husband closely as she lit her cigarette.

"They'll run you out," she said. Her voice was dark and gravelly and danced on Aidan's temples like a migraine. She ashed in the planter. "Brendan won't be in the ground more than ten seconds and Phil will call that vote."

"He can't without me," Aidan said.

"They can count to five. They've been waiting for one of you Mitchells to die."

"They can have it,"—he spat out flecks of cigar—"That old factory means no more to me with Brendan gone than it did when he was alive. Pop left us with every rusty piece of junk he'd never quite paid up on and that there's the last of 'em."

"Yes, well, that may be but I don't like the way this place has marked you, Aid. It's unchristian is what it is."

"Has nothing to do with none of that, Carm. It's this town," he said, looking up the block as though it might trigger a more comforting vision, a hiccup to make sense of Canyon Crossing. But the lights of the town were already extinguished. The farm roads were dark and only the steady east-west drone of headlights along 60 filled Aidan with any kind of relief. Not everyone feels stuck in this place. His head pounded harder and he closed his eyes.

Carmela patted Aidan's knee hard and stood up. "The adventure's been lovely, but we've got more to do on the house."

"Don't kill yourself. Nobody's coming but Beverly."

"Well don't go wasting time on Phil and his lot either, Aid."

Aidan knew he had long since past the point of ever learning what it was you said to the ones you loved to make them go away.

"You look like shit."

"Jackson'll drop me off home. Go," he said. And she did.

BACK INSIDE, AIDAN DISAPPEARED into the bathroom for a long while. His eyes itched and his gut felt like a baseball was wedged in his left side. He sat there fully dressed on the toilet, massaging his side with his thumb, wondering what came next, how it was all going to work out, but he couldn't come up with anything. Then he noticed the scotch bottle still tucked in his coat, and regained his purpose.

As soon as he sat back at the bar, Jackson slid him a fresh shot glass with a nod. Aidan poured his drink himself, slowly, trying not to spill any as one of the old regulars, Jessup, switched stools and slid in next to him.

"Christ, what is it?"

"Never seen *her* before," Jessup whispered close enough that Aidan could smell his warm dog breath.

"Course you have, Jessup. *Jesus.* Been married to her for thirty-seven years."

"Not Carmela, Aidan, *her.*"

Aidan followed Jessup's gaze. Standing with her gloved palms on the jukebox glass, as invading a vision as any hiccup, was a tall stranger in a long dark coat ringed in white fur. With each line of Dolly Parton's Appalachian twang, the woman swayed her hips, letting her head tilt from side to side. She never let her hands leave the jukebox. Aidan thought her hands alone must be summoning the music.

My mistakes are no worse than yours, just because I'm a woman, Dolly sang, struggling to be heard over the crowd.

"Why you figure she dressed all in black?" Jessup whispered in Aidan's ear.

"Why don't you ask her," Aidan said, swiveling his stool back to face the bar.

"Maybe she's going to a *funeral*," Jessup said, savoring this last word.

"Yeah, Jessup, she's saying goodbye to that limp johnson of yours. Leave me be."

Jessup crawled off his stool and Aidan watched as the town's oldest bastard walked over to the stranger. Moments later, old Jessup left abruptly without a word. Then the stranger unglued herself from the jukebox and her silhouette floated toward Aidan so deliberate and lithe that Aidan was reminded of his favorite movie, *Vertigo*, the scene where Kim Novak comes down the hotel hallway once she's completed her transformation for Jimmy Stewart. This new stranger was Aidan's height, maybe taller, and for a brief moment he both wanted her and hated her intrusion.

"What can I get you, ma'am?" Aidan heard Jackson say.

"Tanqueray and tonic," she said, her voice deep and resolute and tickling the musty air the way his wife's lower octaves did. A smoker's voice.

"The man that was sitting here," she hoarsely whispered to Aidan, "He a friend of yours?"

"No ma'am."

"That's good. I wasn't very kind." Jackson placed a

lime wedge on the lip of the stranger's drink and placed the cocktail on a napkin. With the back of one black-gloved hand, she pushed up the gauze that encircled her black pillbox hat and raised the glass to her lips. Aidan stole little glances at her over his shoulder. The lines on her neck aged her somewhere in his own neighborhood. Who was she?

"You don't live around here," he said.

"My, you're a sharp one," the stranger said and sipped again.

"Nice get up," he said, lips disappearing as they pressed into his teeth. He didn't want to look at her and yet he wanted to charge straight at this bluff, this hiccup's bluff. Mourners would be coming from all directions for Brendan's show tomorrow, but not tonight, not this early. It had to be his wires getting crossed again. The woman said thank you, but it sounded muted and faint and Aidan half-expected her to fade out like in the movies or crack open, swarms of swifts flapping and shitting and breaking all the windows. Aidan would play along for the moment.

"You and all the rest of them," he said. "You come here to dance on Brendan. I get it. He screwed a lot of women in a lot of places. The man was a shit. I'll give you that. But you're a day early for those fancy dreads. I passed it by Father Ryerson and he said there'd be no midnight mass for our mother-trucker."

"I packed in a hurry."

"Did you even know him?"

151

"Yes."

"I don't know why anyone who did would be anywhere near this place."

"I knew him," she rasped, her lips cracking a smile. "Once upon a time I knew all of you."

The boys in back cheered loudly at their game.

"What's that?" Aidan asked, leaning closer to her.

She pulled off both of her gloves and laid them neatly on the counter. Her hands were wrinkled with little splotches and trembled a little as she stroked the white fur of her collar. "I knew you, too, Aidan."

"No ma'am. I don't think so."

"It's true."

"Now listen here. We Mitchells have known plenty of folks, but there isn't a single woman he and I both been with, you understand? You come to get a piece of *him*, that's your business, but don't go dragging me into it."

"It's not like that," she said, stroking one of her earrings and massaging the back of her ear as she sipped her cocktail.

"No one's dragging anyone, Aidan. Listen. Pop was the one that always dragged Brendan, wasn't that right? Then Brendan dragged you and on down the line, you dragged your little brother, too."

Aidan's arms alit with gooseflesh at the thought of his brother Christian. He swallowed more scotch. If this was just in his head, why couldn't he turn it off?

"Sometimes, though, it was you and him doubling up

against pop and Brendan. Isn't that how it was?"

Aidan narrowed his eyes and felt the scotch slosh in his head. "What do you know about Christian. How dare you? Fucking hiccup." He reached for her hat and the gauzy curtain encircling it like a cloud.

"Hiccup?" she said, swatting his hand away with strength that surprised him. "What's a hiccup? Aidan, to be perfectly honest, I—"

"Honesty is never perfect, lady. I don't know who you are or what's going on in my head, but why don't you take that stupid hat off and show us your face. That'd be a perfectly honest start. Okay?" He grabbed at her hat again and again she moved his hand away. Then she obliged, removing several pins from the hat and pulling it off. Her straight black hair fell straight and limp as drapes around her cheeks. She snapped her head up and looked straight at him.

Her face was unremarkable, long and plain with as many lines around the mouth and temples as Carmela had and just as much makeup on her thin face to suppress the same vagaries of age. Her eyes were tender and green but seemed to change colors in the twinkly bar light. Something was off with one of them, too. Her right eye had been matched for color but was made of glass and reflected the light differently. *The eyes*, Aidan thought, *were the one piece of our clunky selves that stayed the same size from cradle to grave.* The stranger's eyes held him in their orbit for a good long while. Then with a sudden intake of breath, Aidan leaned back and the lines disappeared from his brow. How did she know the Mitchells? How did she know Christian? *This is something different*, he thought. *This is no ordinary hiccup, but I'm going to have to ride it a good long while to find out.* He let her talk.

"You remember when Brendan turned fifteen?" the stranger began, leaning into Aidan as though daring him to touch her. "I heard the story. You won't mind if I tell it again."

"Go on," Aidan whispered.

"Pop was supposed to take Brendan scrounging for catfish on Old Meyers Pond with the tackle box uncle Abe gave him. Only one of the guiding belts at the factory ripped off its shaft, killing Tom Geiser in a split second and lacerating Jimmy Widmore's face so bad he nearly died, too. You remember all this?"

Aidan nodded.

"Pop went off to Amarillo to be with Jimmy because that's what you do, that's what one *did*. Only he was supposed to go fishing with Brendan for Brendan's birthday and, understandably, Brendan was upset. Wicked and restless that kid was. He didn't want to wait until pop was back. Who knew how long that would be? Could be days. Brendan certainly didn't want to wait to go fishing or for permission to use the pick-up either. He'd been driving it since he was ten after all, earlier than you learned. He also didn't care about the mud track between Old Meyers place and the ranch, didn't care that it could throw you and stick you and that there wasn't much you could do about rescuing yourself without a tractor or waiting 'til summer."

Aidan slurped his scotch and lit another cigar, knowing there was no shutting off the valve now. "Proceed," he said through puffs of his cigar.

"With pop gone away, Brendan was even more determined. He dragged you headfirst into his scheme, roped his brothers in with the promise of Hershey's and a peek at one of those dirty magazines he kept hidden in the baseboard. But you were always a little more cautious than he was. You got to thinking what it would be like if ma or pop found out you'd taken that pick-up. You said if it was going to be one of us gets in trouble, it might as well be all of us. You bounced around the house, exploding into the room you shared with Christian, said put on overalls and get some lures. It'd taken you all morning to find worms enough to fish with and you all knew you'd be spotted by someone in town if you went to buy some.

"Wasn't the town we were worried about," Aidan said. "It was Ma."

"How old was your little brother then, eight? He was excited and scared, but he didn't really have to go. You dragged him into that one. *You* dragged *him*. Three rods and room for three in the front, but you and Brendan made your poor brother sit in the cab to keep things from bouncing off. The two of you whooped and hollered the whole way, telling him what you'd do to him if any of the equipment broke. You laughed as the truck jerked and heaved in the mud and he struggled to keep things put. When at last you made it to the pond, and your brother vomited from the ride, you laughed. When he asked about poison oak out there in the tall grass where there was nothing of the kind, you snickered and pointed at the way he rolled up his overalls to the top of his thighs, watching and shaking your heads as he stood on his thin white legs at a spot along the pond's murky shallows, fishing with the quaint delicacy of a girl."

"It wasn't like that," Aidan said under his breath.

"You didn't even notice when he wandered away, did you? Y'all went fishing in earnest. Your little brother fished far enough away from the two of you he'd be out of striking distance and so he could keep his pocketful of lures a secret. You remember what happened? You remember what happened next?"

"Get out of my head," Aidan said finally brimming, chest heaving.

"You remember how much fish you caught, Aidan?"

"We didn't," Aidan mumbled.

"Not a one?"

"Mosquitofish. Mosquitofish is all we got," Aidan said. "Little silver suckers, small as guppies and limp." Aidan suddenly knew the point of the stranger's story and he knew what she wanted to hear, what his hiccup wanted to pull from the deep recesses of his brain: "You know the ending," he said. "Christian caught all the big fish."

"Christian?"

"That's what I said." He thought she'd go by now. He thought he had released it.

"How'd he do that?"

"If you know, then why are you asking me?"

"There was a trick he had, wasn't that it? A trick to catching the catfish? Tell me. I'm an old woman and I've forgotten this part of the story."

"You haven't forgotten."

"What was it? How did he do it?"

"Earrings," Aidan said. "He used ma's earrings."

The stranger stroked the back of her own ear again. She was playing it fake and over the top. Aidan hated fake and over the top.

"That was it, wasn't it?" she said. "Caught so many it was like the fish leapt straight out of Old Meyer's pond and into the little grass basket lined with newspaper."

"Something like that."

"And what happened to them."

"Brendan threw them all back."

"No, the earrings. Did he lose any of them?"

"No." Aidan remembered Brendan cutting the fish apart, slicing their bloody mouths open one by one until he found the missing earing. Brendan making Christian suck the fish gunk out of the earring to clean it. Made him suck out those fish parts until he threw up again.

"You boys get in trouble?"

"Damnit! Stop it!!" Aidan cried and the bar turned briefly to notice the old man, then ignore him. Aidan shut his eyes. He wished that the woman would trickle out of his brain the way all the other hiccups did. But as he counted to ten, he could see in his mind's eye his father coming toward Christian, striking him and striking him with the back of one cold callused hand. He could see Christian's burnt cheeks streaked with tears and Brendan and he just watching, saying nothing.

There was a rush of cold air as Phil Gilchrist Sr. came into the bar, kicking his boots dry and waving one big bulky hand when he saw Aidan. Aidan stood up. Sweat had returned to his brow and his eyes welled with tears. The stranger was still on her stool. He didn't want to be boxed in by her or by Phil.

"Aidan," Phil said, slapping Aidan's back. "What's the matter with you? You're white as a sheet." The din of the bar began to ebb from Aidan's ears. Flaccid and faint, Aidan barely heard as Phil introduced himself to the stranger, jostling her hand up and down as though he were back switching levers at the factory. She introduced herself as Lillian. *Lillian.* It was a name that summoned little from Aidan's booby-trapped memory. But wouldn't that name have to be familiar? How could Lillian or anyone in this town know so much about Chris?

"What's the matter? All of *you* are the matter," Aidan spat. He stared downward, not wanting to look at anyone for the redness in his eyes.

"Aidan you're upset. I was just across the street and thought I might find you here. I want you to know how sorry I am. Carol and the boys and everyone, we're so sorry for your loss."

"Thanks, Phil," Aidan said, sitting back down to remove the hand from his back.

"Now, no hard feelings Aid," Phil said. "If you need anything, the board's only too happy to help."

The board, thought Aidan, *will be happy to help me buy my own coffin.*

Aidan was surrounded by the hard stool beneath him, the wood bar pressing into his ribs, the strange woman from out of his head who called herself Lillian and dusted off memories of his brother Christian he hadn't seen since— when? Christian had ghosted that town. He wasn't fit for it. He was a sissy, a draft dodger lost in his own jungle. A coward. Aidan felt as though all the eyes of Canyon Crossing were upon him. He snatched the bottle of Blue Label and leaned his scotch breath into Lillian. "You staying here in town?"

"Yes," she said.

"Good. You must be at Gail's place, then. The Canyon Lodger up on Fourth?"

"That's right."

"Get your things. We're leaving. I have lots of questions and I ain't going to ask them standing in front of this *prick*."

"Aidan, you're drunk," Phil said, almost laughing. "What's going on? Don't leave, I just wanted to talk."

"Yeah, well, I thought I did, too, bucko. I thought I wanted to talk to you about a lot of things, like Monday's vote or how the hell you intend to keep my father's factory from shutting its doors. But then"—he looked over at Lillian—"then I don't know."

"What, Aidan? Then *what*?"

Aidan gripped Lillian's hand. "Forget it, Phil. Save it for tomorrow."

THE CANYON LODGER CONSISTED of a long narrow parking lot with plain squat rooms on either side, most vacant that time of year. By the time Aidan and Lillian reached it, it was past eleven and had begun to snow for real this time. The office lights were off and there were only two cars in the lot, a beat-up blue station wagon Aidan recognized as the owner's and a large Trailblazer with Oklahoma plates, both now speckled in little white flakes.

"Rental?" Aidan said, knocking on the SUV's back window.

"Yes," she said, following Aidan's gaze to the license plate. "Flights were cheaper to Oklahoma City. I drove the rest."

"You came here from where exactly?"

"New York. I flew in this morning." Aidan blinked, his mind tripping over the subtle familiarities of Lillian's features, the way she rolled the start of the word *morning*, and of course that one good green Mitchell eye. He'd have to tell Carm more about these visions. This was turning out to be a doozy.

Aidan wandered toward the office, but Lillian pulled him back.

"I have a key, Aidan. It's alright."

They stepped carefully through the accumulation of wet and worthless slush toward Lillian's room in the far corner. Inside, they took turns using the toilet and then they went about pouring themselves scotch in little glasses.

"What is this business about Christian?" he said, sharply, almost soberly. "I want to know what you're doing here and what you know about him."

"Everything," she said, her voice low and resolute, her hands no longer trembling.

Aidan stood up. "Then where is he? Brendan's dead and this has got to be the seventh or eighth funeral he's missed for our family since—"

"Sit down, Aidan. Please."

"My back is shot to hell and it hurts to sit on a bed like that. Tell me what the hell you're doing here in my head!"

"Relax, Aidan." She pulled a pack of American Spirits from her purse and lit one.

161

"Where is he?"

"There was Canada for a long while. Montreal's east end to be precise. I think you know that part. From there it was New York but *he* is not really anywhere anymore."

"Quit circling those wagons, lady. What is it you want?" Despite the swigs of scotch his lips were dry and spittle clung to the corners of his mouth in little white dots.

"Did Brendan ever tell you about finding Chris in Canada?"

"No. We didn't talk about *him*."

"Why?"

"Is this a joke? Did Brendan put you on to me before they pulled his plug?" Aidan shook his head at the ceiling. "One more prank to make me lose it?"

"This is not a joke. Jesus, Aidan, don't you see it? I'm not some spook. I'm not in your head. Brendan was furious with me. Angry I dodged, angry I wasn't there when cancer got ma. In 1972, the very day Brendan finished his last tour, he boarded a train in Amarillo with nothing on but his crisp uniform. He didn't have a single bag on him and he set off by way of St. Louis or Chicago, I'm not sure, but it must have taken him a week. But it was Montreal he was heading to. You told him where I'd gone to."

"I told him nothing," Aidan garbled.

"You knew. You had to have known."

"That's right. I told Brendan how to find that son of a bitch. What does that matter now? He was…dead to us. I don't believe in the resurrection."

"Brendan found me. You know that. You know what he did to me?" She held one hand in the other and squeezed.

"So you *hurt* each other. A long *time* ago. Whatever he did, whatever it was, it's over, ain't it? Whatever this is, it's over. Tonight I'll close my eyes and tomorrow Brendan goes in the ground. Then that factory full of Mexican boys will march right into Phil's hands. And that's for the best. I think I'll get used to these cursed little hiccups. I better, because they are going to cushion my blow. Like a giant pontoon, they're gonna float me right on down into the big canyon." Aidan coughed and hacked, his throat burning with acid. His bloodshot eyes filled again with tears. He sat on the bed, then rolled to his side but his spasms only worsened. Lillian moved next to him and began, tentatively, to stroke his back. Aidan's coughs turned to shallow wheezes.

"Take this jacket off. You're burning up."

He sat up to let her strip off his coat and his thick plaid flannel shirt.

"If my wife knew I was here with you," he chuckled.

He sat listless and barren in a white undershirt, thin from over-washing and with stiff yellow stains in the armpits. Lillian could not help but take in the tattoos— emblems of his unit, thickets of roses, tigers and monkeys and big-breasted women, all of them a faded blurry green beneath the forest of hair.

Aidan followed her gaze to his arms. "I didn't get these

over there," he whispered. "I was clean as a whistle when I got back, unlike most. Brendan took me where he got his—a joint in Wichita Falls with the hillbilly music going. It was a dive little parlor just outside the base where all the air force guys went. It took a full week to do them all. When we were home and the bandages were off, when Brendan saw all the things I put on there, he went at me like an animal, thought he was going to cut me right back open again and let all the ink run out. Or make me suck it out. You see, I'd put your name right next to his. See? That old dog was mad as hell."

"You're the same, Aidan."

He stared at her green eyes long and hard.

"You had to go. *Jesus.*"

Lillian sat up from the bed and walked over to the bureau, playing with the empty drawers.

"I told Brendan you'd come back," Aidan said. "That was at the hospital. He was already too far gone. He didn't say anything, but I think he heard me. I didn't know how, of course. Or when. I see it now. I see you now. I didn't see it at first."

"I thought you might, Aidan."

"It's the eyes. The eyes have it."

Aidan found his legs and stood and clapped his hands. Lillian turned to face him.

"Maybe you came here to share scars with someone, but that game doesn't work with me. Well, actually there *is* no game because, by the looks of it, you've already won." Aidan seized his flannel off the other bed and put it back on, fumbling with the buttons.

"I don't understand."

"You come here to tell me you got out of this whole mess? You come here to tell me you escaped and got to live the life you wanted. You want to rub that in my old dirty face, in the only place I know to call home? Well fuck you, Christian."

"It's Lillian. It's Lillian now."

"Yeah, well, fuck her, too."

"Aidan," she cried out, but he was already gone, crossing the parking lot and marching like a fumbling giant through the storm.

THE NEXT MORNING, AIDAN awoke naked and sweaty on a cot upstairs from Jackson's Saloon, stiff sheets and a heavy woven Mexican blanket kicked to the floor. The room was a familiar refuge and the sound of its radiator hissing in the hot dry sauna of space felt like he was being born into an alien room. His headache was on simmer, his bladder burned, and the heaving of his alien lungs was the only other sound. Outside was the sharp migraine brightness of sun and snow and Aidan shielded his eyes from the small port window. He dressed and pissed and crept downstairs.

A boy, no older than sixteen, with bronze skin and a close-shaved head was sweeping the floor. The chairs were up on their tables, the stools stacked neatly on the bartop. There was a sense of order. Aidan's dulled ears could hear the young man's headphones from across the room. When Aidan was close enough to the door, the boy startled.

"Mr. Mitchell, I didn't recognize you."

"You work last night?"

"Sure."

"Let me ask you something," Aidan yawned. "You see a tall woman? Old, black dress, fur coat. Anyone like that?"

"No sir. I was in the back mostly, watched some of the game, but…"

"How late was your shift?"

"Jackson let me go maybe ten, ten-thirty, after the snow started. I didn't see anybody like that, Mr. Mitchell."

"That's alright. Tell your father I say hello. Tell him he owes me twenty bucks."

"What for?"

"He knows what for."

"Yes, sir."

OUTSIDE, AIDAN SWATTED SNOW off his favorite bench and sat down. The cigars in his pocket were crushed and damp and there was nothing left to light, nothing to smoke. He searched his jacket and felt instead a large bulge in a cargo pocket on the outside. Very slowly he pulled out a knit red scarf. Carmela's scarf. He smelled it and it still smelled of her, the faint stench of spice and impossibly soft. He didn't remember taking it. Had she left it in the bar? Had she asked him to hold onto it? He couldn't remember. He wrapped it twice around his neck and inhaled deeply. The snow made everything quiet outside in Canyon Crossing and it continued to fall and fall.

Aidan was not there yet, but he could see himself frozen at the lectern of Brendan's funeral, trying to summon the things which should be said as you stare out at your brother's coffin. Aidan imagined a frozen world outside the mortuary walls. Hardened glaciers in the gorge, swifts dropping from a slate sky like stunned missiles dotting the snow in one long perfect V, pointing south. When they moved the show to the grave at the cemetery, the levers on the coffin would jam and an icicle-faced Father would shrug his shoulders and give his blessing.

Or Aidan could clear his coarse throat and talk of another brother, the one that got away and got a chance at rebirth, because that story might knock some of those fat fucks off their narrow pews. Aidan had a rough idea of how it could go and he chortled to himself alone on the iron bench outside Jackson's. Carm would laugh, too, he thought, but wouldn't our stranger in the fur coat need to be there? Wouldn't he need her to make that bucking bronco picture on the flimsy easel complete?

Aidan practiced a new eulogy to himself.

It was hard to miss the sound of his own red pick-up's snow tires as they crunched and squeaked their way to a stop outside Jackson's. The truck jolted the way his father's truck once did, the one from that fishing trip all those years ago.

"You look like shit!" Carmela yelled as she rolled down the fogged-up window. The truck idled and belched. "Gail's got rooms. Why'd you stay in this dump?"

Aidan stood up slowly, his muscles screaming. He walked around the pickup and got in.

"Is that my scarf?"

"I like it."

"You need a shave, Aid. You need to show those sons of bitches what you're made of today. Where's that scotch bottle you were sucking on? One shot of that and a shave and you'll be right as rain." She drove steady and slow down Second.

"Bottle's gone. Finished. Hey, I know what I'm made of, Carm."

"Oh yeah? What's that?"

"Snips and snails and puppy dog tails," he said. "Here, Carm. Turn left. I got to check something."

She made the turn without question. "You're all upside down, Aid. Your daughter's been asking about you since they got in last night."

"Turn right here. Why is Beverly upset?"

"Why is she ever upset? That deadbeat she's with probably. You even finish your speech?"

"Gonna wing it."

Carmela spat out the window. "I suppose that's what he deserves. What can you say about a man like that?"

"Not much Father Ryerson's going to let me say. I have something else in mind."

"Where are we going?"

"Pull into the Lodger for a minute."

"Why?"

"Just do it, Carm."

She turned the car and the back wheels jangled a bit on ice before straightening out. On instinct, Aidan craned his neck to make sure nothing had shaken loose from the cab in back. It was empty but for a bed of snow. Carmela put the truck in park and they sat idling in the lot.

"Is it those visions again? Have you been seeing things?"

Aidan stared at the SUV from Oklahoma and the lit, curtained room beyond it. Nothing stirred in the corner window but a single shadow which dimmed the lamplight as it moved. He waited for a door to fling open, for the same flock of swifts to fly at him and splinter off, searching for grubs beneath the fallow fields of snow, all those acres of white draining into the canyon. How he wanted to fly there with them. But the motel door stood strong and still on its hinges. No birds came.

Aidan sat blinking and breathless, quiet as the canyon, watching for Lillian, watching and waiting for her shadow to stir again.

SUICIDE WATCH

Quentin Compson made suicide look tidy in *The Sound and the Fury*. The plans and letters, the broken watch, roaming the streets to psych himself up, the bridge with no witnesses, all of it. Civil, almost.

I was never any good at it. In high school, after AP study group and when no one at home was expecting me, I used to drive my tiny Honda up PCH, past Malibu and Ventura, practically to Santa Barbara. I drove as fast and far as I dared, until the emptiness of the dark mountains, the stars hidden by pollution, seemed to match the coldness of the car with the window down, the vibration of the stick shift in fifth. Sometimes blasting music, sometimes not, I always found myself numb and dreamy the drive north then hot and sweaty, often crying, the way back. The pain was a dull roar, chest pushed up through my throat, all the way so my pupils ached and I thought there was no way I could ever do it. That is, come out of the closet, not only say I was gay but restart life on new terms. Catastrophe awaited every path on that map.

There was one spot, near Pismo Beach, where the freeway banked sharply left so, if you didn't follow the curve, there was a gap big enough to break through and, with enough runway, launch efficiently to the ocean boulders below. There'd been an accident some time before, so the barrier was wooden planks then, not steel railing or even those concrete pylons they sometimes put up temporarily. But it never really synced up, that curve and the peak of my melancholy. There were always too many cars around, the distant twinkly lights of L.A. too pretty for such a scene. Back in 1984, the summer the Olympics came to Los Angeles, there had been that other car crash too, the one with mom that my brain still hooks on, the Bronco that ran over the front of our car, then flipping, flipping, memories like scummy foam that keep bubbling to the surface, and which I spoon away, but which keep bubbling up again.

I suppose what happened was I wasn't comfortable with witnesses. I picture two boys, curious, just woken up from a nap on a long drive down from visiting their cousins in San Francisco, their faces plastered to the back window of their parent's station wagon, a single car-length ahead of me. They would be the last people to see me alive if I went through with it, a memory which would haunt them until old age, when the pain of their own bodies became too much to bear, when even if the image of my silver Honda sailing over the cliffs was remote enough to be dismissed, their arms would still alight with gooseflesh whenever they heard about a car crash, and they would feel that same loneliness without a name.

There was a more serious attempt junior year with a fistful of Benadryl. If you draw a bath and do it there you drown, but my father and stepmother were listening for late night baths and things out of the ordinary. Plus, my little stepbrothers were always around. So it was late at night in bed when I tried it, and all that happened was I woke up hours later with my dad screaming my name, slapping me hard, a pile of pink polka-dot vomit soaked into the sheets beside me.

I knew I hadn't the courage for the hard stuff: guns, razors, rope. But like Quentin Compson, I knew the geography of bridges. There's an especially high one near the Port of Long Beach that lots of people use, but the logistics of getting down there and finding a place to leave the car always seemed too complicated. And eventually that curve near Pismo got fixed.

The new therapist is much better than the first one. She avoids all that curing stuff the creepy guy in Pasadena tried, all his energy wasted trying to pray it away. So much kneeling on old carpet. Now that I'm at N.Y.U. and seeing someone in a walkup, with a view of maple trees that have shifted color over the course of the year-plus I've been with her, it all feels more legit. Dr. Helen Weisman is like a tiny bomb bound up with energy. I like her thick Brooklyn accent, her honest face without any makeup, or made up to look that way, the silliness of her moth-eaten sweaters several sizes too big that she constantly pulls back up over her shoulders to emphasize a point. She'll sit with her legs crossed and power through a bag of M&Ms over the course of a session, constantly calling out the bullshit stuff my brain floods me with. Her office is all exposed brick and narrow and we sit so close together she can poke my shoulder for emphasis. Shift out of that, she'll say. Stop, close your eyes, where do you feel that in your body? And I can actually feel the knots unfurling as she prompts these little shifts of thought, training my brain and my body another way. These shifts I recognize as tender lurches in my left side, just below the ribs, a soft twitch. It feels like it's just one butterfly now and it is dying, but it knows it, and it's okay.

THERE IS A QUOTE I WANT to lead my class essay with. It's Quentin reciting the words of his father in *The Sound and the Fury* which reads: "Time is dead as long as it is being clicked off by little wheels; only when the clock stops does time come to life."

I have so many other thoughts I can't quite organize yet. That and this tacit agreement I've made with myself to come out somewhere strategically in its pages. Not sure yet if I'm doing it for Dr. Helen Weissman or myself, but maybe I'll get an 'A' from Professor Gehry who will think it brave. Or maybe because of the title of the essay—"Suicide Watch"—I am ensuring a conference with the dean. A title like that has lots of meanings, but the administration is already on edge about the bodies that keep piling up in the marble atrium of the university's 10-story library.

I FIRST MET PROFESSOR GEHRY in a brownstone off Washington Square, a week before term. His office was so dark, the professor's hand so cold when he shook it, I thought he was trying to suck the summer warmth from me. Over the course of our sit, I was distracted by his bottle-blond hair and large perfect teeth, the way his smile pushed his cheeks all the way back to his ears. That and the annoyance pulsing in his jaw, a sense of impatience with me or disappointment, a look I'd seen before in the lingered gaze of my mother's gay friends, adults expectantly waiting for an epiphany I hadn't yet arrived at.

We talked about the outline for the term, the ideas I had for an essay from the basis of the syllabus and the books I'd already read. Or not quite read, rather, the movies I'd already watched based on the plays of Tennessee Williams. A half-knowledge. Marlon Brando's pecs in that t-shirt, Vivien Leigh's wrists and diction. But not the subtext. In conversations with older gay men like Professor Gehry, I felt like I was forever slipping, not able to tell the most basic of jokes, or relate in any way that broke the tension, a sense that I'd traveled very far to visit a foreign country but forgotten the basics of the language I had prepared.

"That poster is striking," I said at the first lull, remarking not on Oscar Wilde in his fur coat and cane, nor the photo of droopy tulips from the Mapplethorpe exhibit, but the picture of Virginia Woolf in a fur coat. "So mannish and grim," I said.

And there, a shudder of disappointment in the professor's shoulders, his forehead wrinkling in pity or disgust.

"I read your application essay."

"That's embarrassing. I didn't know they showed those to anybody after a certain—I mean, I'm a sophomore already."

"I ask for them because I find the earnestness of high school writing fascinating. Really, it should be studied. You moved here from California?"

"Don't count it against me."

"There's a spirit in your prose. Truly. It surprised me. I don't usually see that much right brain in a business student."

"Right brain?"

"Creativity. Art. Your words did this little pas de deux. There's a cleverness there, but in other places you trip and fall flat. You need editing, structure, but when it works, there's a rhythm. I don't know how to describe it. An assonance? Anyway, what am I trying to say? Your proposal for the term…"

"On *Suddenly, Last Summer.*"

"Yes. Forget it. It's going in the trash. It's thin. I'd almost say trite. I think you need to tackle something deeper."

"Okay?"

"Where are you on Faulkner?"

"I've read a bit. Some stories in high school. *As I Lay Dying, The Sound and the Fury.*"

"Good. That's a base. Eddie, this is your growth edge. Leave Tennessee Williams to the theater queens. Believe me, they'll be insufferable without it. Let's get you through Faulkner and then you'll be ready for mannish and grim."

The professor looks behind him at the image of Virginia Woolf, pausing with what feels like a feigned reverence.

"Have you read *Absalom, Absalom!* yet? Make sure you get a first read of that under your belt right away and we'll figure out the angle on your paper."

THOSE FIRST FEW WEEKS of Gehry's class, I found it hard to concentrate in the room. I got stuck on things, like how the Brown Building is haunted by its own special heat source. Not the south-facing windows, not the radiators, nor the suit I wear to class, but literal ghosts on fire. Burning bodies. Their heat rises through the linoleum. It wafts in from vents and through the porous brick. The heat is so thick I can see it sometimes undulating in waves before the oversized windows, as though something is ready to take shape before my eyes.

They cut that part out of the tour. They don't tell parents of prospective N.Y.U. students about the Triangle Shirtwaist Factory. How could they? How would it go? If you look up there, in the upper floors, right where Johnny and Susie will have class one day, you can see where one hundred and forty-six garment workers (nearly all women, some as young as fourteen) either burned or leapt to their death right here where we stand. The tour guide, at this point, would have to whistle the bodies all the way down for effect.

What started it? Do they even know for sure? An oil lamp knocked over? A cigarette? Or just the accumulated heat of stitch-pedal-stitch. Stitch-pedal-stitch then whoosh. I've read the wardens locked the doors from the outside, a common practice. There was no way out and only one impossible choice for everyone inside: burn or jump.

Burn or jump.

That was in the early 1910s, nearly eighty years ago. Now there are child labor laws and mandatory breaks for factory workers. In all these old buildings now are fire escapes and push-to-exit doors and fire sprinklers. *Death shakes up the landscape of a city*, I've jotted in my notebook, not sure how I'll use it.

I got both excited and repelled by the professor's energy, like magnets flipping between poles in my stomach.

Different than the twitch beneath my ribs, this energy made me squirm, made me shift in my seat, made me want to run away. I wanted to bury myself in the worn gravel of the professor's voice, but I didn't want eye contact, and I certainly didn't want to be called on. Professor Gehry—Patrick, he insisted his students call him—could see right through my suit, right through to my tight chest and heaving heart. Straight through to the ghosts.

The rest of the class was Tisch. Film students and actors, dancers and critics. It was odd, the seeming newness of their sundresses, their polos and board shorts, the dirty heat of summer still bright on their Midwest necks. No one there was from California.

Did anyone else feel the heat of the ghosts the way I did? Did Professor Gehry in his beard and leather riding chaps, vest, and visor, in his shit-kicking motorcycle boots and black SILENCE = DEATH t-shirt? Was that uniform he wore for class even authentic, or was it a performance like the actor kids in class? I couldn't tell. Silence equals death. ACT UP. Fight AIDS. I'd only recently learned what that meant.

"Eddie Donnelly, let's start with you."

"Yessuh!" I half-shouted, the word coming out with a weird southern twang I hadn't expected, as though the southern drawls of the other students' readings in class had wormed their way onto my tongue. *Yessuh*. Some of the other students looked back at me and giggled.

"Thanks for joining us, Mr. Donnelly. Again, scheduling first conferences. Back of the room to front, starting tomorrow at 10 a.m. That work for you?"

"Saturday?"

"Yes, imagine that, working on the weekend. What a world. Does 10 a.m. work? I'm in a much better mood for the first conference than the last one of the day."

"Yes. Ten a.m. tomorrow, Saturday. Your office?"

More giggles from the class, another detail I'd missed, or language I was unprepared for.

"Under the Hangman's Elm. In the park."

"Okay," I said, pretending I knew, nodding. Like everything then, I was winging it, hoping to pick up the rest from context.

IN ASTOR PLACE, THE SUBWAY began to scream from the southern end of tunnel. I stood perilously close to the edge of the platform, looking down at the third rail and the rats still trying to find refuge somewhere. I took a step back only when I saw the panicked look on the conductor's tired face, his arm on the emergency brake as he ushered the train to a stop. There was a *Daily News* piece not long ago. They say the conductors know the key to spotting a jumper is the jumpers watch the tracks, not the train.

There was a line I found to put in my essay. I'd have to look it up again. It talked about how *Absalom, Absalom!* was Faulkner's answer to his rival, F. Scott Fitzgerald. The character of Colonel Sutpen, in other words, was Faulkner's answer to Jay Gatsby. Faulkner was saying that in America, the so-called "self-made man" doesn't do it for passion or love as Fitzgerald would have you believe, but out of a primal need for competition and the red-hot spite one carries for those who've wronged us. For Colonel Sutpen it was his childhood memory of being treated as poor white trash by a Black butler telling him to go around back. This self-made man, the Sutpen kind, his motives are jealousy mixed with pride, a sense of grievance tightening into vengeance, and he doesn't give a damn what he destroys along the way. Meritocracy is just stealing everything while no one minds the store. Same attitude that says to lock the factory doors, make girls and women work until their fingers bleed, and if they're careless enough to let the oil rags catch fire, there will be others who'll get it right. If they don't want to burn, they can jump. The window's right there. But if you use your body to break the glass, we'll charge your family for the damages. Colonel Sutpen would recognize that form of capitalism.

Burn or jump.

And something else to add there. For my essay. About Southern culture and how it was shaped in the decades after the Civil War. About that sick and twisted form of grievance where even incest is more acceptable than, in Henry Sutpen's words, a drop of nigger blood. About how this is no different than now, with Pat Robertson going on, this idea that suicide or drug overdoses or disease—self-extinction as it were—is more acceptable than living with a single drop of faggot AIDS blood in the national stockpile.

By the time I got to my father's building uptown, his town car was already double-parked outside.

"Eddie!" he barked from the back window. "Get in."

"Where are we going? I have to piss."

"We're going to be late!"

"I'll hurry," I said, running into his building anyway. The condo was a mess, and there was a small shit already in the pot when I went to use it. I pulled my shirt over my nose and flushed, realizing as I looked at my reflection that my notebook was no longer tucked under my arm. It was gone.

I searched the hallway, my clothes, every stray shelf I passed on my way in. It was nowhere, not in the condo, not in the first elevator down or the second one I took back up. Nothing left with the doorman and if I'd left it on the subway, it would be gone forever. What would someone make of it, my notes for class, my ramblings on suicide and Faulkner, on ghosts and coming out? Could any of it be traced back to me? Or if I was indeed notebook-blind in that moment and it was still there in the cubby of one of my father's bookshelves, was that fate? Was that me willing it there so that my father would find it, read it, and I didn't have to be the one to tell him I'm gay after all?

"Where have you been? Jesus, Eddie, we're going to be

late."

"I lost my notebook somewhere," I said as I got in. "I have a conference tomorrow with my professor—" I started to explain but Dad was already pulling the car phone from its cradle and dialing.

"Where are we going?" I mouthed silently to him, settling in as the driver pulled back onto Seventh to head back downtown. Dad held his finger up to make me wait.

"Hey, Frank...Yeah I'm seeing it tonight," he said into the phone. "He does what? You're full of it. River's just one of these brooding James Dean types, that's all. Girls love him, he's not a fag." He said that last word as naturally as all the others, still avoiding my presence, his body hunched over a cigarette as he lit it. "Yeah, I'll hold."

He took a long drag, blowing smoke out the window, then pointed to a small black bag on the floor between us. "That's for you, bucko. For your birthday. Open it."

I unearthed a small black box from the bag, opened its stiff lid slowly to reveal an expensive silver watch. The red-tailed hawk in my throat divebombed to my stomach, landing, fluttering its enormous wings. *Time is dead as long as it is being clicked off by little wheels; only when the clock stops does time come to life.*

"Frank—Frank, listen to me. I don't care. We need him for the Bradbury thing and we need it to be mainstream. I'm not getting in bed with the fucking you-know-who's again, not this funding round. You'd have to put a gun to my head if—no, Artie, Artie! Not that way. We only got time for pizza, head to John's in the village so we can grab slices. No Frank, I'm talking to the driver. Eddie's here."

I'd put the watch on, testing how it felt. Dad handed me a flask and two glasses out of a slot in his door then whispered, one hand over the mouthpiece: "Pour us a little, will ya? That watch looks good on you, yeah?" Reflexively, I looked at it, checking the time against the green numbers on the driver's dashboard. The watch was fast.

"Uncle Frank says hello, by the way. Yeah, I'll hold."

"Why are we headed downtown? I just came all the way up here."

"Sorry, bucko. Shit came up and this film I gotta see is only at the Angelika. By the time I figured that out I knew you had already left. Relax, I tried calling you!"

"What movie then?" I asked, but I was playing dumb, because I checked the Voice listings every week, expecting Dad to call for work, expecting him to want my youthful "take" on something, which is only him wanting to hear so he can decide for himself.

"*Private Idaho*," Dad said. "Super arty according to Frank but maybe it'll be good… Yeah, I'm here. Of course he's doing well at N.Y.U.… No, he's in the business school… Because he's great with numbers you fucking idiot. Yeah, he takes film classes. Producing ones, I told you that… Just like the old man. Except I'm getting more pussy," he said, pinching my leg hard.

THE LINE AT THE ANGELIKA was thick and full of talkers. Inside the cramped theater, the thrum of bodies was just as dense. We managed two seats along the aisle but far back from the screen. There was no square inch of space anywhere. It was as though the theater was triple booked. I realized there were mostly gay men around, but dad was oblivious. He checked out every woman, head to toe to head, as they passed him in the aisle, then he whispered a number from one to ten in my ear. I could smell his Marlboro breath.

In line for popcorn, I played with the new watch. It bit the hairs on my arms, but it was handsome. It looked good there, if only to give my arm the appearance of weight and depth. Quentin Compson smashed his grandfather's watch on his dresser, pulled the hands off so forcibly they cut his finger. This thought made me thrust my hands in my pockets.

Ahead of me were two men shoulder-to-shoulder. The one in the jean jacket whispered something in his friend's ear. His eyes were blue-grey, his nose long and sharp. He caught me staring and I looked down. After they paid, one of them spun around and said, in a florid Southern accent not dissimilar from the actors in Professor Gehry's class, "Does your mother know you're seeing a *lavender* picture?" and before looking up to respond, I realized the stranger was talking to another young man, not me. They all hugged, squeezing shoulders with an intimacy I found shocking and intoxicating all at once.

"Three dollars," the old lady with pink hair said to me after I order the popcorn, pronouncing it *tree*.

Dad grabbed kernels from the bag before I even sat down. He was engrossed in the trailers which had already started. In a little while, he'd pull a notebook and pen out of his breast pocket and jot stuff down. Going to movies had always been work for him. I thought of my own lost notebook and felt nervous about the conference tomorrow. I was so unprepared.

The film started. River Phoenix alone on a country road, muttering to himself. He was so young, so beautifully hippie handsome it hurt. I knew, because I'd done the math, that River was exactly one year, one month, one week, and one day older than I was.

River looked down at an old pocket watch, absent its chain, something that looked like an heirloom. Visions appeared, as though he was high or in a trance. Clouds moved in fast motion, salmon leapt upstream, a barn fell from the sky. I rubbed one finger over the face of my new watch, testing how much pressure I could place on the glass. Goosebumps pimpled my forearms, my heart started to dance, worrying what Dad would think of the movie, wondering if I would be able to withstand it. I decided then and there I would tell him I'm gay as soon as we were outside. Finish it. Rip the band-aid off! A new life beginning in three, two, one. A new resolve stiffened my whole body, down to my feet on the concrete floor, then gradually relaxing. So simple, that directness.

Gay hustlers, or men who simply made money that way, seemed impossible to me until I saw young men like these outside the bus depot my first year in New York and realized how they must afford clothes and drugs, a roof over their heads. Keanu Reeves was a hustler, too, but I wasn't as taken with him as I was with River. My gaze upon him was undeniable and I wondered briefly if Dad could tell, if the men sitting behind us could tell.

Dad left an hour in, picking up from his chair as though going to the restroom but never coming back. I kept looking back at the double doors expecting his return. He'd be pissed off, leaning over to pinch my shoulder as though to say, "for fuck's sake let's get out of here," as he sometimes did when he hated the movie. But he didn't this time. I had to sit with the uncomfortable desire to seek him out and yet felt drawn in by the film, not wanting to leave. Wasn't that a kind of coming out as well? If I stayed and Dad realized why?

In one scene, Mike (River) and Scott (Keanu) are unable to get Scott's motorcycle to turn over. They make camp, some remote roadside prairie. Sitting by the fire, Mike finally confesses his love for Scott, something that has clearly been building throughout the film. Mike mutters his desire into his knees as he sits hunched, unable to look Scott in the eye. He wants to be with him, to kiss him.

But although Scott loves him as a friend, he doesn't feel the same attraction back. I felt Mike's heartbreak, pushing tears back and barely able to breathe in that stuffy theater full of bodies. Then Scott offered himself up to Mike, to come and lay with him by the fire, to hold the space with him as his friend, to sit with him in mourning the loss of a relationship that was not to be.

What would it be like in Faulkner's story if Quentin's roommate Shreve had offered such solace, an acknowledgment of unrequited love but still the enduring bond of friendship? Would Quentin still be alive?

I waited until the credits were over and the lights came back on and the fourth wall broke at last. I moved slowly because of the crowd, but I was ready. No matter what Dad said, I would bull my way through it like Uncle Frank. There was burning and there was jumping, but there could be a third way. I could stop the clock and make time come alive.

I waited for him on the stretch of Mercer Street where Dad should've been or at least the car should've been. And my nerves started to come back. The restlessness and anticipation burned so hot I wanted to peel my clothes off. I summoned the courage to walk up to a group of men lighting each other's cigarettes to bum one off them. A man in a brown corduroy jacket and dark jeans, a thin mustache, read me instantly with a squint. He offered the lit cigarette from his mouth, not letting go as he held it to my lips to inhale, laughing when I coughed the marijuana smoke out.

"Thank you," I managed, my face warm with embarrassment.

"Anytime, sunshine," he said, looking back at his friends then looking back at me, his head cocked to one side to size me up.

I checked my watch. It was 10:08 p.m. The perfect minute we'd learned about in marketing class, the time they use in all the watch ads. Either 10:08 or 10:10, because of the perfection in the balance of hour- and minute-hands in that configuration. The kind of detail you learned and then can't stop seeing in magazines and billboards.

"He's not coming," one of the voices said behind me. Then another: "They never do."

The man with the joint placed his hand on my shoulder, squeezing it tenderly the way Dr. Weismann did sometimes. "Go on now and find someone new. You deserve it."

When I began to cry, the stranger and his other friends instinctively took a step closer. I recoiled, nearly tripping over the curb, stumbling a little then bumping right into Professor Gehry, who smiled with recognition.

"Eddie? Are you okay?"

"Not nice to keep a girl waiting," one of the strangers said.

"I don't do virgins," another one pretended to whisper. "Shit's a mess."

"Mr. Gehry. I mean, Dr. Gehry. I'm sorry, I—"

The professor looked over at his lover, who was clean

189

shaven, a natural blond, and younger than the professor, maybe late 20s, the drawing of a shirtless sailor emblazoned on his shirt.

"Eddie, this is my boyfriend Alex. Eddie's in my Southern Lit class."

"Nice to meet you," I said, as if by rote, not sure if it even came out correctly.

"Are you here with someone?"

"I—was. I was here with my father. He's gone now."

The professor and his boyfriend shared a look. Was I joking?

"What movie did you just see Eddie?"

The words didn't come out. The name looped in my head like a mantra, but I couldn't get it out. "The River Phoenix one. My father left halfway through, so—"

"Do you need to talk for a bit?" the professor said, one corner of his lip rising, so sincere it hurt. I knew I should say yes, that to walk with them and tell them stories about Dad, about how I was ready—right then!—to come out, could be everything, but I couldn't bring myself to accept.

"No. Thank you. I'm headed back to my dorm. Some other time," I said and walked away. I couldn't look back.

WASHINGTON SQUARE PARK WAS eerie that night. Rastafarians casually offered weed for sale—*smoke smoke*—and students talked by the fountain as though they had something to say. Older folks walked dogs. It was too late for children.

The professor was right. The Hangman's Elm was indeed magnificent, especially at night where the valleys of its crusty bark seemed deep enough to stick your whole arm through. Some say it's the oldest tree in Manhattan.

I stepped over the black chain so I could take a seat within its roots, hug them to me as I watched the park. And then, even though the professor wasn't here, it was as though I had the conversation with him anyway, with the ghost idea of him anyway.

Why is it so hard to say? I imagined saying, to start. And he would say something pithy, something like *Giving birth to a thing is never easy.* And I'd tell him how I ruined his evening and he would tell me that he lived close by, in the mews, that he and his boyfriend trusted each other. And I would confess right away that I'd lost my notes on the subway and I wasn't prepared for tomorrow, and he'd just reassure me that it was okay, that it could wait. There was time.

And it hit me again, the loss of my notebook, and my eyes welled with tears again, running my hand along the root of the elm as though to unburden the pain. Although, if that truly was the oldest tree in Manhattan, then it was the kind of thing that persisted even there, despite the pollution and all it must have witnessed. George Washington's cannon practice. Lynching. Buildings going up in the name of progress. Fifth Avenue when traffic went straight through the arch. Late-night muggings, rapes, murders. From its highest branches, the black smoke of death billowing from the Asch Building, now the Brown Building, as the young factory workers burned or leapt to their deaths. Later, the rush of the fireman's hose spraying the upper floors. Even when the spray of water is to put out scorched bodies, it makes a rainbow in the midday sun.

If Dr. Gehry wanted to know what I had so far, to distract me as I circled what I wanted to say, I would say *I get it now, having read both books with Quentin Compson.* The Sound and the Fury *and* Absalom, Absalom!

I would say how the tension between Henry and Bon is the same between Quentin and Shreve. In his retelling of everything, Quentin embellishes Henry's story, especially Henry's conflictions about his stepbrother, because Quentin is processing and, unintentionally perhaps, mirroring the perverse and unspeakable conflict he sees in himself, that is: the desires Quentin has about other men, maybe even his roommate Shreve, just as Henry may have had about Bon. This business about Henry's protectiveness over his sister, even incestual lust for her is a bit of Faulkner's—and by extension Quentin's—misdirect. Quentin is fucked up by his sister, too. But Henry is not so much jealous of Bon because Henry covets his own sister, but rather it's Henry's self-love, a love of himself as a man, that disgusts him, certainly nothing he has words for or understands yet, certainly not the racism mixed up in his disgust of Bon, something so mixed up and broken in him he may think he's the only one. Until that moment at the end of the novel when both timelines converge, when Quentin and Henry meet. It is quite possibly the only truly authentic moment in the whole book, bright with the white-hot burn of being seen. The shock of it! Of course Quentin commits suicide later.

And even if it was hard to follow, Dr. Gehry would say something reassuring. Give me points for trying. Because Faulkner's tough. It's subtle. He'd say *You must really know yourself for that reading to come out the way it did for you. You must be a real thinker. Listen, you want to come out of the closet? Great. You don't, that's okay too. There's time. But only someone who's walked through it or contemplated walking through it—deeply—gets that book.*

Cobble-stoned Greene Street runs along the Brown Building. I don't know how I ended up there. Was I following the ghost voice of the Professor? Above me, a large purple flag snapped and billowed in the wind. It had N.Y.U.'s emblem: a torch. A torch outside a building where bodies burned.

There, that choice again.

Burn or jump. Or, somehow, stop time.

The sidewalk was new. Fire hydrants have been replaced. Only the cobblestones remained, these tiny gray coffins. Did the women who jumped break their necks here? Or was it closer to the line of the building? Do you leap and jump out or do you fall straight down? How long before the blood washed away? A single season of snow? Could you tell from further up? Or does it take zooming out to see the pattern?

I circled the building until I found the green light, the one that meant there's a security guard, an officer, someone safe in case you were being attacked. And the door was open but there was no one at the station and so I took it as a sign, permission to keep walking, slipping unnoticed into the stairwell. Was it time? Had time stopped?

A dull fluorescent glow in the stairwell, my sneakers making squeaks on the marble. Two stories, five. Already out of breath. Eight stories. How far up were they? Ten stories? Eleven? I didn't have the strength to look down the gap in the stairwell, to give myself the vertigo induced not from the height, not from the fear of the height, but from the fear of falling. The fear of that temptation to let myself fall, which is what I wanted and didn't want at the same time. But the gap was too narrow. It was impossible there.

I tested the door at the top of the stairwell, inching it open. There was only a red exit light in the hallway. No voices, no steps quickening their pace to catch me. At the end of the hall, there was a window where I gathered my bearings, figuring out which side faced Greene Street, so I could pinpoint where the fire began.

Only one room was unlocked. It was empty. Not even a piece of stored furniture there. The wooden floor had been buffed to such a pristine shine it reflected the city lights streaming in from the bank of latticed windows. It was like stepping out into air.

As I crossed to the far windows, I could see the honeycomb screen like a net placed just beyond the glass were it ever to break. Suicide proof. And not a single panel would open. And, as if to prove one final point, the ceiling was veined with red pipes, so many sprinkler-heads the room would flood in seconds were there to be any kind of fire.

I stepped up into a window well.

I stared out at the horizon of city lights for so long it felt forever before I was able to look down. The vertigo came, but not so intensely I couldn't stay with it. With a shock, I felt remnants of the stranger's pot again, catching up to the high.

Where were all the ghosts now? Where was their heat?

There is a story my mother told every Fourth of July. How when I was two, I climbed the couch on the second floor of our home by the Silverlake Reservoir to follow a bird I'd seen out the window. It was summer, they were having some wild pool party, and all the windows in the house were open. There were window screens, but an old kind, only held to the sill by a little triangular latch. Before anyone realized what I'd done, how quickly I'd climbed on the couch, or how the latch that held the screen to the sill came undone, I was gone. Whoosh. The way mom told it, she leapt down in a single jump shouting every curse word imaginable. I was rushed to the hospital, but they could find no cuts, no broken bones, not even a bruise. Children don't tense up when they fall from windows the way adults do.

I TRIED TO LOOK DOWN AGAIN, pressing my face into the glass to see if I could see the street. These garment workers, did their gingham dresses billow in the wind? Were they already on fire? Would there be any beauty in their fall, any beauty at all?

I had to look away but, as I did, I caught the glow of my own eyes in the window's reflection. Only I saw it the way my roommate Rob would see it, like a perfectly framed shot for one of his student films.

A few weeks earlier, that first week in the dorms, there was a heat wave so intense the building lost power. We lit candles anyway, despite the R.A. telling us not to. We didn't care. We played cards, opened the window as far as it would go despite the noise and clamor of Broadway. The room was so stiflingly humid we took off our shirts. And there was this moment where I found myself staring at the way the candlelight flickered in Rob's eyes, the way his smooth, shaven cheeks, and his sweaty torso glowed flush and innocent. One of those Quentin-and-Shreve moments full of sexual tension. His face was mesmerizing, and maybe Rob understood completely what was happening. I am certain he did and, like Scott in the movie I'd just watched, he took no offense. He neither indulged nor rejected the moment. Rather, he told me to stay put and brought out his home camcorder to capture whatever it was he was seeing in my eyes, a depth my brain didn't allow yet but a cinematic moment Rob's did.

Time coming to life.

If I held my breath, I could hear the new watch on my wrist. The ghosts were still there, but not as hot as they once were. And quieter than they had been. I knew they lived on in stock photographs, in a plaque they placed outside, in the union marches and chants each spring.

The most terrifying word in that phrase—burn or jump—was not the verbs but the conjunction. Or. A deliberation. Agency, if only for a moment.

Either burn or jump. We cannot stop time. And yet we can persist, reliving a present moment of being seen, like Quentin at the end with Henry, living forever in a sense of timelessness not clicked off by little wheels.

I had to write it all down. Build out the essay while it was still fresh. Prepare for the conference with Professor Gehry the following morning. Out of habit, I reached into the inner pocket of my jean jacket, clawing deeply into the place I was sure I'd already checked, or else ignored because I didn't realize it could fit so neatly there.

And the notebook was there. And my pen.

Because it had always been there, waiting for the right time.

GO TIME

Ray's buddy Martin loved to golf on Thursday mornings because there was no open play. His club had higher dues and so was less crowded than Ray's. By the time you finished your round, the special at the clubhouse was a Reuben and they made a damn fine one. Ray knew all of this already, but Martin pitched it anyway over the phone, his voice on the line accentuated by his periodic crunching of ice cubes, the kind he liked to plop in his post-dinner champagne.

On the news, they warned of thunderstorms colliding with a haboob. "I don't want to go out in that," Ray said, watching Leo floss standing before the television in their bedroom, his husband's unblinking eyes scanning the animated weather maps.

"Everyone is always making it out to be the next apocalypse," Martin said. "They do it for ratings. And for Christ's sake say *sandstorm*. *Haboob* makes you sound like a fool. If the world is coming to an end—which it isn't—we'll have the best view from the club."

THURSDAY MORNING THE SKY was indeed bleak. Purple-gray storm clouds in one direction, a copper-red haze in the other, like two great blobs of paint mixing on the palette. The light was out at Magnolia and Ray sat in traffic watching the young crossing guard, sturdy in his uniform, fat biceps and white-gloved hands pushing impatient cars through with graceful ease.

Ray's big brother had taught him about disasters. The big ones that killed tens of thousands, sometimes millions. When it was go time, people's lizard brain kicked in. Fight, flight, or freeze. But Ray's brother called people seekers, fliers, and sticks. Seekers were drawn into a thing. Not all of them heroes. Some were drawn out of only a dazed curiosity. Or a well-timed opportunity. Fliers were the opposite. They were drawn away. The willingly evacuated, the newly orphaned, those whose fear of the thing often meant never returning, disassociating from all time and space. Sticks, on the other hand, were neither drawn in or out. They burrowed down right where they were. Suicides. People waiting for god. Stubborn codgers watering their roofs. Going down with the cabin as the volcano erupts.

Watching the crossing guard's face as he passed—the poise and concentration flaring in his jaws—Ray knew he was watching a seeker, a person wholly different than himself, a flier if ever there was one, foot poised on the gas to punch it at any moment. Leo, or Martin's wife Eileen, they were the sticks, unfolding chairs in the church basement, removing the clock batteries, sipping from a flask so they'd be crispy enough at the edges when the time came.

THE CLUB'S PARKING LOT was empty so Ray could easily spot Martin's Mercedes by the entrance, his expired handicapped tag still hanging in his rearview. Inside, Ray found Martin already in the dining room, sitting by the large picture window with a view of the distant storm. On days they golfed together, Ray and Martin were content to dress like twins, both in white sneakers and knee socks, khaki shorts, colorful club polos just loose enough to cover their well-earned guts. Today Martin was navy and Ray was maroon.

"Sandstorm my ass. It's a little *weather*," Martin said, rising to give Ray a hug, their bodies like leather punching bags knocking together as they patted each other's backs.

"That thing's headed this way, Martin."

"Don't believe the hype. Sit down. I ordered drinks. Tell me, was Leo as crazy as my wife was this morning? I mean, she left her *purse*. She *never* does that."

"They opened the basement to make room for people... caught up in the excitement."

"What they're caught up in is fire and brimstone. Those thumpers have 'em by the short and curlies is what that is. God I wish we could be out there on the green! See that flag at the first hole? It's not even windy yet!"

A siren rang in the distance as an ambulance flashed past along Country Club Drive.

"Uh oh, another house on the market," Martin said, winking and clinking his ice water to Ray's, then swallowing half of it down, to get at the ice, to chew through it the way those giant Arctic machines must do to get to the world's last bit of oil. "Jesus, what's taking them so long?"

The bloody marys came after a long wait, tall pints with long skewers of pickles, peppers, olives, and cheese. Ray hadn't told Martin yet that he and Leo were taking a break from drinking but he supposed the pending apocalypse was a special occasion. Ray stirred the lava of his drink for a long time before taking a long steady draw. It was strong and delicious and so loaded with horseradish Ray immediately pressed his nose in with his palm to extinguish the fire.

"I don't get what you see in that, friend," Martin said under his breath, releasing a burp into his fist as he tiled his head in the direction of the new waiter, a gangly kid with long blond hair pulled back in a ponytail. "Runty little dicks flopping about. Hairy asses. You actually want to do it with something like that? I mean Leo's rugged-handsome, I'll give you that, but that kid looks like he learned to shower this morning. You smell that Irish Spring? God!"

"Do you want to sleep with every woman you see, Martin?"

"No, but I *think* about it."

The waiter circled back with two slips of paper with pictures of golf clubs.

"What now?" Martin said, impatiently taking it from him.

"Sorry for the intrusion. It's a list of restricted titaniums."

The text was small and they both reached for their glasses.

The gist was that certain titanium golf clubs were causing grass to burst into flames when the clubs were swung. Two fires in California had been blamed on them already. "You have some of these, Martin. The Winstons, right?"

"So what, I can't play with them now? Can you even imagine if our strokes were wild enough to start a fire? Whammo! Whoosh! Ha!" Martin's laugh turned into a wheeze.

Ray looked out at the sandstorm. The curtain of dust was a dozen miles off, maybe more, dragging its way along the suburbs north and east of the city. The golf flags had begun to stir to life, but there was no dust. Maybe Martin was right, maybe they could get a round in. Then a rumble of thunder vibrated the room and Martin's drink slipped in his grip. He caught it before it spilled completely, but it was Ray's turn to laugh.

"Horse shit. It's all horse shit," Martin mumbled, licking red drops off his fingers. "You don't believe in it do you? God's wrath and all that? Please tell me you don't because if you do then you go on ahead and stick your ostrich head in that church basement with my wife."

"The end will come, Martin, but not on a *Thursday*."

"Ever look at an actuarial table? Better than any goddamn religion on the market."

"It's their preacher. Leo never shuts up about him. I think it's his voice they want in their head when things get rough. I mean, between you and me, I don't need that blow-dried hair flopping all over the place to tell me the world is ending."

Martin clinked his glass to Ray's and they promptly sucked down the rest of their drinks.

"Eileen thinks Yellowstone will blow any second, destroy the whole Northwest."

"Leo's son lives on the Oregon coast and he always asks if he knows his evacuation route for a tsunami."

"I suppose it was only a matter of time before our wives freaked out about Arizona. But the odds of something like that happening *today*."

"Millions do die from disasters, Martin."

"They die every day of everything else. You want to know what keeps me up at night? The hospital. Antibiotic-resistant organisms. Twenty-five thousand deaths last year and the numbers keep rising. Don't you go in for your valve thing next month?"

And that's when they saw them, the great fireballs of light raining down and zapping the ground the way an alien spaceship might in the final assault. The clubhouse had begun to populate with other stubborn men anxious to tee off, all of whom stood now and watched as buzzing orbs pelted the fairway with intensifying frequency. Then the strange lightning concentrated on a single target—a small wooden outpost the size of a small trailer, a storage shed most likely—which exploded in a burst of flame. Gasps of shock vibrated through the crowd as everyone stepped back from the windows. They were summing up their surroundings—the roof, the double-paned glass, wondering what would withstand another onslaught, if it came. When the wall sconces flickered and died, that was it. The dark clubhouse threw everything into deep relief. Silhouettes of old men pulled cash from their pockets then fled.

Martin and Ray stayed put, entranced by the exploded shed whose smoke the wind was now clearing from the debris. Only a tall black bucket remained, golf clubs poking out from its top. Martin began to say something, but another ball of lightning struck this final remnant and the golf clubs themselves caught fire, a birthday candle on the green cake of grass.

"Must be the Winstons?" Ray cracked and Martin began to laugh, quietly at first, then with an ecstatic wheeze which overtook him until he had to drink the rest of his water to stop and catch his breath. The lights in the clubhouse came back on. The surge was over or there a backup generator.

The waiter returned with sandwiches and a second round, noticing the fairway fire for the first time.

"What happened out there? Someone said—"

"Lightning, it's just lightning," Ray said, turning to Martin as he caught him stealing a scalding hot french fry. "It's not like it's the end of the world."

Martin held half his Reuben to his lips. There was hunger in his eyes and his open mouth was ready to receive, but a marked solemnity began to spread through him. Was it a prayer he felt coming on, or fear? Ray watched as his friend licked at the Russian dressing oozing from its sides and then dug in, with eyes closed, richly savoring it.

They continued to eat in silence as the clubhouse emptied out, watched as firemen sifted through the rubble of the shack, spraying the ruins with white foam before climbing back into their red RV.

"Let's go somewhere," Martin said, tossing his napkin onto his plate.

"Nah, I've got to get back." Ray could already feel the alcohol in his head, the large yawn coming on. "The dogs will be going crazy and there's stuff from the yard I should bring in if it's going to get worse than this."

"No, you're coming. Leo and Eileen are going to be locked in that basement for hours. Your dogs will be fine. You and me, we'll make our own fun."

There was no arguing with Martin. As soon as he stood, trying to signal the waiter to settle up, Ray realized he was too tipsy to drive. He thought then of all the fliers fleeing disasters and how they must inevitably collide with seekers on the road. Did they pass each other without speaking? Certainly people would make their case, wouldn't they, convincing others to swim against the tide of their lizard brains?

Outside the club, the buzz of discharged lightning electrified the air. Ray could feel the same buzz of nerves that radiated out from his clavicle, down his arms and to his fingertips, the excitement he felt as a child following his brother into the woods—from the intoxicating scent of cedar and pine, the supple moss grip of the trees as they felt their way in the dark. No matter which body Ray was feeling more, his seeker body or his flier body, Martin was leading and it helped to have someone ahead.

THE HIGHWAY OUT OF THE CITY ran southeast, away from the storms. Martin's car was comfortable and quiet and whatever unease they might have felt at the club seemed to subside as they got further away. Martin placed his hand tenderly on Ray's chest. "That calm you're feeling right now?" Martin said, "I call that the coefficient of actuarial bliss. The odds of something bad happening are always lower than what our gut says. Start to recognize that and you tip the whole goddamned machine over. You fall asleep as the plane takes off, you swim lazily in sharky waters, pitch your tent on the lip of the goddamn volcano."

Martin fiddled with the radio but no station came in clearly. He switched to a CD. Phil Collins was singing: "*I can feel it coming in the air tonight, oh Lord...*"

Ray was calmer now, it was true, but still found himself drawn to the window in search of signs, evidence of the great cataclysm his brother always warned about—abandoned cars or scorched trees, a pack of neighborhood dogs gone feral.

"You think God really cares about the faggoty stuff?" Martin said, turning the music down.

"The gay stuff, you mean?"

"That's what I meant. Do you think He gives a flying fig? Eileen and I talked about it and we don't think so."

"I hope not."

"Say, you gamble right?"

"I go from time to time. Leo doesn't like to. Makes him anxious. I scored pretty big a little while ago, not sure if I told you about that. It was one of those two-deck blackjack tables where it's easier to count cards."

"You can do that?"

"I play a good game."

"You'll sit on my right then. I'll follow your lead."

Ray realized in an instant where Martin was headed, keeping the car pushing eighty the last twenty or so miles to the Spirit Lake Casino. Ray could already feel the cards in his hands, taste the free drink a handsome buff waiter would bring.

At the highway exit, though, the casino's three-story monitor that usually advertised the latest entertainment and all-you-can-eat buffets was blacked out. The sky had turned dark again and all the traffic lights were out, too, wobbling in the wind on their metal arms. Traffic was lined up ominously in the other direction and a great sucking sound made its way through the vents.

The Spirit Lake property—a hotel and casino, a gas station and mini-mart, an enormous parking lot—was set back a half mile from the highway. A fire truck blocked the main entrance and only from there could they see the roof of the hotel on fire, billowing orange flames that licked wildly at a growing cloud of black smoke. Hundreds were evacuating. Sirens wailed. More fire trucks and sheriff's cars poured onto the scene.

"Jesus, Raymond, look at that. You think some hotshot was on a streak in there, breaking the house and had to stop?"

"You quit while you're ahead, Martin, that's the trick."

Martin turned to face Ray. "Horse shit! You play the *odds* and when the *odds* are in your favor you *stay*."

One of the firemen began approaching Martin's car, angrily waving his arms for them to move. Martin U-turned quickly and sped away. Impatient as always, he drove the gravel shoulder to pass everyone lined up for nothing.

Many honked but no one blocked their way. He regained the highway, but traffic was slower there too and Martin couldn't find a rhythm, not with his Plan B off the table. At every exit he came to, he pulled off, driving a lap of the side streets.

"What are you looking for?"

"Some place open for a drink. Some place with tits we can ride this thing out."

So it was a thing now. The storms, the strange lightning, the casino fire. For the first time, Ray could see the odds in Martin's brain being recalibrated. He was watching things more closely now. There was still nothing on the radio, no signals on their phones. Their spouses might very well be padlocked in the church basement, holding their tongues out for cyanide capsules.

"There's no bar out this way," Ray said.

"Sure there is. I've been to one. It's got a Bond-girl name like Honey Rider's or Pussy Galore's or something. I just have to find it. It'll be open, it's *gotta* be. I mean, you don't mind a little shaker show now and then do you?"

"If it will get us off the main road," Ray said with a shrug.

Only there was no bar, no strip club, and they were forced back on the highway after all. Traffic sputtered to a halt on the final slope into the valley and they were stuck. The city had disappeared from view, swallowed by the sandstorm, a billowy brown wall like a mountain on the move that was fast approaching. Ray leaned forward and in the small thread of sky still hanging on to blue, two falcons soared above, their bellies striped white and brown, wings majestic, like the ospreys that stalked the river for fish in the Oregon of Ray's youth.

"Why do you hang out with me, Raymond?" Martin said, jabbing him with his elbow. Ray was looking at the thin blade of river winding its way through the gorge off to the right, seeing if all the animals were fleeing, if new fissures in the earth had opened up. Wind and dust whipped in all directions, enveloping them in a copper cloud. The river disappeared, as did the cliffs on the other side of the gorge. Visibility shrunk to four car lengths, then three, then two.

"Leo and Eileen schemed us together, remember?"

"I know *how* we got pushed into the golf thing. But why do you keep coming back?"

"Huh. Maybe I've never told you. You remind me of my brother."

Martin's grip on the steering wheel eased.

"I didn't know you had a brother. Is he as handsome and charming as me?"

"Will always had about three girls going at once."

"Had? Where is he? Tell me he's still around and we can get into trouble."

"Sorry, Martin."

"Damn it, Raymond. It's always the good ones! I'm sorry. What was it? Don't tell me. Lung cancer! You know that's half a million deaths last year? Leading cause in men and women. They keep finding melanomas on me, you know, scooping them out one after the other, but I know there's a bigger C out there. I know the odds and lung's got the best."

Ray wanted the traffic to move. Ray willed the dust to clear so they'd see another exit ahead and could do one more search for a bar, a Mexican joint, anything. But everyone seemed settled in for the long haul. Car engines were off, seats leaned back for a nap. People honked once or twice to get it out of their system, including Martin, but otherwise it was eerily still.

"Martin, I'm sorry," he said.

"For what?"

"The melanomas. Leo's had those before and we sweat it every round. But Will—"

"No, I'm sorry, I shouldn't have—"

"Let me finish. I've been trying to say that Will didn't die of lung cancer. He drowned."

"Shit," Martin said, honking the horn long and hard. "Fuck!"

"It was a long time ago. He was seventeen, I was ten. Death by misadventure."

"What did you say?"

"The coroner's report. It said death by misadventure."

"Don't ever say that. Lazy insurance salesman like Bob Fucking Pensecola say *death by misadventure*. All *life* is misadventure. There's no *death* by misadventure. There's death by—Jesus!—we control so little of it we might as well forget we control *any* of it, isn't that right? You certainly don't need to *pray*. That's what I wish Eileen would understand. This all happens anyway, all of it, to hell what we want."

Sweat pooled in Martin's armpits, beading on his temples. Ray began to feel swampy himself. They checked their useless phones again. Martin wiped his brow with the bottom of his shirt. "This is a cluster, a real fucking cluster."

A large insect landed on the windshield with a loud tap, then a second. Green beetles with red streaks along their backs. Martin turned the wipers on and they flitted away just in time.

"How'd it happen? With your brother I mean."

The cloud of dust thickened, its burnt, ashy scent already finding its way through the vents. Faint echoes of sounds came this way, too—dogs barking, a girl screaming to test her lungs.

"The river by our house," Ray said. "He and his girlfriend."

"Jesus," Martin said, swallowing hard. "Was it like a suicide thing?"

"No. That is—we don't know. Not for certain. There wasn't a note or anything."

"They just go for a swim or what?"

"We grew up near the Willamette, the main river that cuts through Portland. Lived there with our mom a few blocks from a park right on the water, kind of place people took their boats to launch from. These days it's all kayaks and standup paddle boards. Back then some fishing scows and canoes, once in a while a speedboat. We'd had record rains the previous winter and now it was spring and Will wanted to see how high the river had crested. We knew it was already up to the seawall, but there was a chance it was breaching the seawall and flooding the park. I heard him talking on the phone to his girlfriend and since it wasn't raining all that hard, I snuck out after him."

Ray paused for a long time and the two of them stared forward as though waiting for something to happen. Martin reached behind his seat for two bottles of water and handed Ray one. He cracked the cap on his and took a long guzzle. Then Ray did the same.

"You were there?" Martin said.

Ray nodded with a great inhale, having to stifle a cough from the mix of dusty air and water. "You know how people say when bad stuff happens, that time slows down? Well I remember it going quickly. I was throwing on my galoshes and coat after he left. I was chasing after him, taking the alleyways so I would beat him to the park, hide in a hedge and scare him. I loved to do things like that, especially to his girlfriend because she had this crazy squeal that made me laugh. I beat them there, and it was eerie. It was as though the night and the river had swallowed everything. Parking lot underwater, the great lawn underwater. I hid behind this hedge just beyond the waterline, where it was still dry. They showed up a few minutes later, my brother and his girlfriend. I was going to scare them. But they started to get it on—kissing, whispering in each other's ears. They shared a joint and felt each other up. They stripped their clothes off. I was—I was so embarrassed. You have this pact with your brother and I'm violating it, right? I'm the one crossing the line and so I pretended I was a mole underground that couldn't see. I knew if I was found out, they'd call me names—a pervert or something—they might even be angry enough to beat me."

"Jesus," Martin was saying, looking out the driver-side window, pushing the palm of his hand into the bags underneath his eyes.

"It happened fast, Martin. I couldn't hear them anymore and when I looked up, they were wading through the parking lot, water rising from their ankles to their knees. Electricity was still on and lamps hung on wires above them. I could see their butts and backs above the waterline and I couldn't take my eyes off their pink skin in the darkness, for fear they would disappear if I did."

"Enough, Raymond! Jesus, I get it. I'm sorry."

Martin began to cough again. His eyes were bloodshot and he reached for another water and drank it all down, dribbling the last bit on his shirt. His chest was heaving and he seemed to look through Ray, past him, so Ray looked that way, too—north and away from all this, this stupid sandstorm, their little Arizona lives, north all the way over Nevada to Oregon, to Portland, Martin's eyes burrowing down into the muddy riverbed where Ray's brother was eventually found.

"There's no right thing," he said, putting his silver wraparound sunglasses back on. "I'm sorry, Raymond. You did what you did. There's no right thing. There never is."

Martin unbuckled his seatbelt and opened his door.

"What are you doing?" The sudden intake of dust made Ray cough.

"I've got to get out of here, see what's what. Stay with the car, bucko. I'll be right back."

And like that he was gone. The door slammed shut, his keys left dangling in the ignition. Ray watched him cross in front of the car, one arm covering his nose and mouth. Then all of him was swallowed by the storm.

Two young boys in the backseat of the car next to theirs stared at Ray. They'd watched Martin go and now they were watching him, seeing what he would do. Was Ray an idiot seeker or a stick? They leaned taut and strained into their seat belts, four eyes like burrowing beasts.

Fucking demons. "Stop staring!" Ray shouted, now wishing the world would crack open if only to swallow every seeker, annihilate the whole race's macho bullshit. That was it, wasn't it? Fliers were just seekers with sense, evolved sticks.

Except Ray couldn't stand being in that car alone any

longer. He gripped the metal release for the door just as a man in a bright orange vest squeezed by. He wrapped on the hood of Martin's car, then another, then another, urging people to get out, pulling the handkerchief around his neck up over his nose and mouth, pointing to it to show Ray he would need one, too.

A parade of men and women, children, dogs, all trained their feet downhill, their faces covered in dust thick as stage makeup. The storm was louder now, thunderclouds roaring north of us and echoing against the unseen mountains. As I finally cracked the door open, there was something else the soundproof bubble of the car had muted, the sound of rushing water, a sound that robbed Ray of all his breath, sharp needles twisting in his stomach.

"*Shall we gather at the river!*" someone was singing, and Ray half-imagined he would see Leo and Eileen, their entire congregation here to be delivered for the final judgment. Idiots, all of them.

Ray followed the crowd in search of Martin. Must they now salvage each other from this desire for destruction? Ray followed the sound of rushing water. The aches in his knees and shoulders flared up, then began to subside as the barometric pressure eased. He felt young again, pregnant with the energy of high-voltage wire.

Every few seconds, a semi rumbled past going the other way, it's heavy diesel engine chortling and cracking, the truck honking as though to celebrate its escape. There was a steep embankment between them and the lanes of traffic headed in the opposite direction, enough to prevent anyone from climbing and escaping that way, although people tried. Ray could make out a line of city buses, dust-dirty faces in their windows. Maybe Martin had already made it on to one of them. Maybe he did have sense enough to fly.

Ray jogged faster then, cognizant of the finite limits of safety out there on the road. The wind had died off, and he could sense what was coming—a monsoon rain ready to dump from the sky. It had already begun somewhere ahead. That was the roar of water they heard. Not a river. Not the dark muddy rush that swallowed Will, but something cleansing, something pure.

Ray zagged left around a car, now running ahead of the others, enjoying the sound of his feet crunching the median gravel, hearing the rain getting closer, feeling light, his frustration with Martin subsiding. When at last they hit the wall of water, the pelting rain slowed everything down. The dust on Ray's face began to stick, tasting like over-steeped tea, a bitter tin-can tang.

Then the spigot turned off as quickly as it had turned on. Ray caught his breath, could even see a break in the clouds, shafts of sunshine poking through. And there, in a patch of sun, was Martin, soaked and miserable Martin, leaning on a stretch of bent metal that separated the road from the plunging gorge below. An excited scream burst from Ray's lungs, shrilly and hoarse like a teenager whose voice is changing, so giddy he was to find him. Martin had lost his golf hat, his sunglasses were cracked. His elbow was bleeding badly and Ray pictured a bird, its wing clipped, no longer able to fly. Martin was crying.

"Martin, you look like hammered shit. Are you okay?"

Ray held him as he partially collapsed then slipped through Ray's arms to the ground. Ray went down with him, an awkward negotiation of legs and torsos so that Martin lay at last with his head in Ray's lap. His breathing was shallow, his hand clutched to his chest and shaking intermittently. Martin's eyes still watched Ray clearly, gripping his hand tightly. Ray screamed for help.

"I have you just where I want you," Ray tried to joke, hoping to crack a smile on Martin's face. "Breathe steady, Martin. The cavalry is coming," Ray said as red and blue lights of emergency vehicles approached from above, their sirens piercing. People were already pointing them out.

"Another house on the market," Martin said, a mix of laughter and more wheezing, the same he'd had all morning Ray was now realizing. Martin rolled part-way over and spit in the ground, wincing as he rolled back. Somewhere behind his clouding green eyes Ray could see the actuarial tables, the odds spinning out into various scenarios and percentages.

Ray craved more rain, craved the oxygen it would bring, anything instead of that stuffy sauna of highway. The sun grew so strong and hot that Martin squinted from the sudden brightness. Ray leaned forward so his shadow kissed Martin's face, shielding his eyes from the sun.

For the first time, he could take stock of the road, see the wide trench a flash flood carved from the highway just a few car lengths ahead. It looked as though dynamite had gone off, several cars and a truck collapsed into the hole, a hole that seekers were now working to free life from. The danger was over, Ray thought, the rush of water now eroding the world somewhere else down the line. The apocalypse had simply passed through, as all storms do.

But then the world in the light of that road became unbearable. The sharp brilliance of yellow blooms in the roadside brush all around was enough to make the body tremble with fear, that the storm had weakened and passed, sure, but Martin was slipping.

The EMTs butted in, Martin's rain-soaked head gently lifted from Ray's lap. Ray was helped up himself, made to sit on the bumper of a nearby pick-up. Several EMTs worked on Martin on the ground while another checked Ray's eyes, wrapped his arm to check blood pressure.

Ray felt woozy, as though the road was tilting slowly toward the hole in the asphalt, like the giant drain of the Willamette River that had sucked his brother down. They shifted Martin's body to a stiff orange stretcher, strapped him in, and lifted his body up the embankment to the waiting ambulance. Ray would be told later his friend was pronounced dead in the street, not at the hospital, but he knew they were wrong. He was certain Martin had waved. Not a big wave, only a subtle tilting of his head, seeking Ray out, lifting his arm to write on the air, the way he would summon a waiter for the check just before tee time.

Ray had tried to stand, to follow Martin, to seek out the next adventure, but the EMT held one hand to his chest to keep him seated. The pressure of his hand on his ribs was cold and hard and Ray felt dizzy again. He closed his eyes. In a flash, the paramedic's steadying hand became the flat ridge of the dashboard in his mom's old car. No, not her car, but the Datsun she borrowed from a friend so they could drive Will's ashes to the coast. There were no working seat belts and at the point where the road slalomed that last hill before you saw ocean, she had leaned forward into the wheel and Ray into the dash, Will's ashes in a canister between then. They watched as lane lines disappeared so frighteningly quick below them, a version of flying. Learning not to be scared of that primal feeling vibrating from his sneakers on the floorboards up to his skull—the one that said there was no higher purpose, no answers, no seeking or flying, or staying put, just gravity and time.

WHAT WE PICK UP

Before I'd spun out of the business for good, I used to sleep with an older poet named Gabriel who told me one night what he'd gleaned from his brief stint working in Hollywood. He'd been a script doctor, one of those spare studio readers they paid extra to jot notes in the margins. In those days I was renting a converted garage detached from its home near the Silverlake Reservoir and my parents' old place. We were skinny-dipping in my landlord's pool, a bottle of wine and pot gummies sloshing our heads, and Gabriel swam up to me, his salt-and-pepper beard dripping with water, his amber eyes wild with the moon.

"Eddie Donnelly, let me tell you something about *those* people. They know very little but they know there can only be two plots in this world. Some say eight, others five, but these crazy-makers have it whittled down to two."

Gabriel cradled my head in his hands, kissing me with the tenderness of a whisper as though I was the hilltop tree he was blowing his wish into. I felt the hair of his legs on mine and could taste the copper hum of wine on his breath. "You know what they are?"

I had an idea but I let him tell me.

"A journey…and a stranger comes to town," he said, drawing it out, as if he was both telling it and hearing it for the first time.

"What's yours, then?" I asked, swimming backward to the shallow end.

"I'm from New Joi-zee," he said, laughing to find his buried accent and the uncommon way it pitched and stretched its vowels between his cheeks. "I'm a strain-juh comes ta town, though you can call it 'fish outta water,' if ya like."

I found my own gravity on the concrete steps and walked the brick rim of the pool to our towels, hugging one deep into my face and chest.

"I was born here. Except for college, I've never lived anywhere else," I said and Gabriel crossed his arms over the lip of the pool, resting his head to look up at my body. With the lights of the dark pool still off, his head and hands were like body parts crawling out of a grave. I found myself shriveled and spent and uninterested in the sex he'd followed me here for.

He grabbed my ankles. "You're *from* here but you're still on a journey," he said looking up at me, suddenly sobered by something he saw or was thinking. He let go and swam away, on his back, staring somewhere into the haze above, a kind of head space he got into when he was composing lines in his head.

YOU NEVER SHAKE THE weird rules of Hollywood, the kind that shape every conversation at every party. Streisand won't take stairs. Spielberg doesn't ride in elevators. Lassie is the first and only animal that, according to her contract, flies first class. And never promise anything to the dog trainers because they're in a dispute with the cable network that, quasi-legally, owns her. Excuse me, owns *them*. Lassie is a whole line of dogs, like cosmetics, a kennel full of well-bred and politely trained collies related by blood to the original who all live on a ranch so far east of L.A., they've forgotten the sprawl. Somewhere beyond the Tejon Pass they spend their days scent-marking and tracking for trouble. Then one of them will be scooped up and limousined somewhere, or flown in a private jet for an appearance—sometimes for charity, sometimes for kitsch. But what happens to their individuality when only a microchip sets them apart? Must they all maintain the illusion they are *that* Lassie? Must all of them keep saving the world?

LONG BEFORE GABRIEL THERE was Jake, who I'd met after

I dropped out of N.Y.U. and moved back. I was barely twenty-one and working as a production assistant—a P.A.—on a commercial job in Malibu where Jake was the Second Assistant Director—2nd A.D. it read on the call sheet. He was the one who ran the show behind the show behind the show. We were shooting on the stretch of Zuma Beach they use in all the commercials, the kind of place where Gidget hung out, where CHiPs leaned against their motorcycles between takes. To scan the horizon, with its perfect cliff in one direction and its long curve of shore in the other, its perfect bathroom shack and outdoor showers for surfers, was to be taken in by the lobby, the spell that kept us all here.

Jake was fifteen years older, a bit shorter and stockier than I was, with a closely trimmed beard and brilliant blue eyes, always squinting, crunched into little black sockets of sadness or lack of sleep. He roamed every moving part of a set with a clinical eye, able to anticipate the most minor of problems before they happened and snowballed up the chain. And because it was one less decision he had to make, every day he wore the same uniform of black cargo shorts, black suede cowboy hat, and a tight black oxford that showed off his biceps and the tangle of tattoos up his arms.

On my way to my car after wrap one evening, Jake stopped me and invited me out. I was surprised he knew my name, but Jake had an iron memory when it came to the details on the call sheets and paychecks. He'd even suggested a bar in my neighborhood, a mixed bar, mostly gay, with an Arabian theme, dark and red and still smoky in the days before they passed a law.

"You're a good P.A.," he finally offered an hour later, over his tumbler of bourbon. "Don't count on it right away, but I take certain people under my wing." People like me, he was saying. I don't remember telling him much about myself except that I was single, maybe that I had a spec script I'd been working on, like everyone else. I didn't tell him who my parents were and if he had suspected or known he didn't say. He sipped his bourbon and let me rattle on about things. I told him how I'd gone to John Burroughs, the school with the wide, brick façade they used as the establishing shot in a million TV shows. How, whenever there was a scene there, I'd pretend the show took place in my school. Like it was someone in my class being busted for drugs. The new kid in Social Studies was the undercover cop. The girl with the biology scholarship, the edgy one with the weird yellow contacts, she was the one the detectives would come to ask questions about after her body showed up in the river.

Jake listened patiently. He'd placed his big hat on the bar beside him so I got a good look at his hair, thick and dark but shaved close on both sides and back. High and tight, the lady told me at the salon when I told her what I wanted. I thought Jake must look like that the moment he stepped from the shower, the moment he first sliced a comb through. I envied that simplicity, the earthy sandalwood smell of him, the warm tickle of his clove cigarette, the poise he exhumed with every gesture.

I could tell he was interested, that I was slowly letting myself forget the most basic rules about not trusting anyone in this business. His was an eager smile, and his eyes lingered on my face an extra second before he spoke. When he got up to piss, he squeezed my shoulder a little too tightly and for a second I wondered if I'd been misinterpreting his gestures all day, like it wasn't code between us but something different. Maybe he belonged to that culty religion I know nothing about except that it's popular with actors and everyone is afraid to badmouth it in mixed company.

But then Jake was back and laughing and starting in on a story about a set he'd worked on recently, the previous month, where a famous actress from *that* religion had holed herself up in a trailer.

"The shoot was running long," Jake said, ashing his cigarette in the tray, looking around to ensure no one was listening. "The producers were upset because lunch was pushed back, and there's that calculus about overtime. We were going to be up to it in meal penalties if our day got any more behind. But she wouldn't come out. The director tried—and he was a charmer—but he came out shaking his head, just like everyone else, even her own hair and makeup people we thought knew her the best. So we break for lunch and wait. We fill in with ticky-tacky stuff and

B-roll and then, about an hour later, this black town car with tinted windows pulls up. Some lady gets out. Older, real put together. Overdressed, like she was showing up for a charity luncheon, or someone's funeral. She doesn't say anything to anyone. She's on her phone, roaming up and down the sidewalk like a lost ghost as she scans the trailers and motorhomes. We're all sort of shocked when she walks right up to the actress's trailer and is let in! And not two minutes later, I swear to God, the lady comes out with the actress behind her, like a miracle kitten she's just rescued from the tree."

"Who was she?" I said, but Jake just shook his head.

"Everything goes on with the scene like normal," Jake continued, winking at me the way he did before, a world of double meaning in it, pausing only to throw back the rest of his drink. "See, I'm the only one who notices she's no longer using her purse in the scene. In all the other takes, she was using her purse, but it was a close-up now and didn't matter. The continuity person hasn't noticed it yet. But I notice. And I wonder where the purse is and am about to call props over when I see the old lady is standing outside the house holding the goddamn purse under her arm, tight as a football—like *this*—like it would be hard to get it from her. And so in between takes I sidle up next to her and say, 'Excuse me, you're so-and-so's friend?' And she looks at me and says, loudly, not whispering the way everyone else does on set, she says in this full-throated uppity tone 'I'm her pastor,' and I say 'Oh, that's great, I just want you to know that so-and-so's character has to grab something out of that in this scene and they might need it.' But when I reach out to take it from her, this cheap little shiny gold prop purse, she hikes it further behind her and tells me that so-and-so has asked her to hold it for her and 'No one can bring it to the actress but me!' What can I do? I tell her thanks and find the producers and we piece it together. That the actress is not part of that religion yet, just giving it a spin—auditing, they call it—and there is something in that purse she needs to keep close. It's a test for her and she can't be parted with it. She'd been hoping to do the scene with it, but the director kept changing how it was going to be used, maybe not at all. So this little talisman, whatever it was, was going to have to go back in her trailer without her, or be fondled by the nasty props guy. So the actress panicked and called her people and that was that woman, the highest-ranking pastor that could come. She held the purse. Like leaving your passport with a concierge. Can you believe it? Those people."

Jake wouldn't tell me who it was, but I felt sorry for her just the same, being judged by everyone on set. I lost track of the story he told me after that, lost in his river of words and the beating of alcohol in my brain. I kept picturing this woman holding a prop purse to keep her friend's magic safe. There was something so tender about it, so simple, that I kept coming back to it in my mind on the long walk to Jake's house from the bar. Even after Jake was fast asleep,

I kept returning to it, wondering if there was someone somewhere who would carry such baggage for me.

I WORKED A LOT OF production jobs before Jake called me again. I worked for whatever I could get. I pulled heavy cable from muggy grip trucks. Got yelled at in my headset. I memorized the stupid rules of each producer. The rule with some is that if you're given an order directly from their underlings over the walkie, you count to ten in your head before you do anything because most of the time, they'll tell you to do the opposite right after. Or cancel.

On sets like these, on location mostly, you spend a lot of time going up and down the stairs of trailers. Knocking and waiting. Inhaling the smoke stench of the producer's motorhome. Carrying out thousands of little orders. Drinking half a bottle of water before losing it somewhere. Getting sharpie marks on your hand. Losing the hair on your arms from grip tape. All day long is blue balls, waiting for something to happen that is over in seconds. You hear only snippets of jokes, only threads of various arguments, and always you have to leave in the middle. Or everyone freezes during takes, not making a sound until the A.D. says, "cut and back to one," then everyone forgets what they were saying before and you start some other thing.

I fell in with the sound guys. Those were good gigs. Sound gear was nothing. Two little cases, maybe three. I could help put the mics on, threading wires up the back of actors' costumes. Now talk at normal volume so we can test the levels. There. That's good. And move your arms around and talk. See if we get a clean sound. Good. And sometimes I tell jokes to see if the actor is primed. If they don't laugh, it means they're ignoring me and focused on their lines. If they laugh, it means it's going to be a long day.

I DID SOUND FOR ALMOST a year until Jake came around for me like he promised. And once I got in with him, I never really worked for anyone else. The money was good and I'd never felt so rich, where it was all my own doing and not my folks'. I was wanted. I could taste what was coming next and it was completely my own. On hot summer nights in that detached garage, which I rented from a retired gay couple forever traveling elsewhere, I'd cool off by swimming naked in their pool, lap after lap, imagining I was going in a single, straight line, just like in the old Cheever story, only in this version I was swimming into a tunnel that would pop out at the reservoir, and then the pool after that, and on and on all the way to the ocean. Wherever I finished, somewhere nice along the coast, some place cozy and minimalist where you could step right down to the sand, there would be that other life. The one I'd waited for.

I didn't care that Jake sold drugs, maybe because I never liked the hard stuff and never saw Jake with it either, and I liked the extra pot I took home for myself. This was years before it was legal and everywhere.

I liked that we worked all over, that the days felt long and varied. For the first time in my life I was leasing a new car, a silver Jeep which Jake made sure to fit into the first scene he could on the show we were working on. He said I could always replay that episode and remember that time in my life.

There was sex with Jake, which was frequent and exciting enough, but sometimes we brought in a third, sometimes one of the actors. Usually this meant jerking off or a blow job, something quick and stolen in a trailer at the beginning of the day or sometimes the last spare seconds of lunch. It was always with Jake's arrangement, though, and always there was some petty cash for me at the end of the night. It happened only once in a while, at first. I'm not sure I noticed when it began to happen more often.

Months like this turned into years. One show went three seasons. And one of the horny nobodies I used to suck off before call turned into a big deal, even won an Emmy for his role as the broody younger brother. Not that they ever talked to you much after.

THE LAST JOB WITH JAKE was in the Mojave. An independent film. The crew was doubled up in cabins, squat little shacks that stood at the foothills of a long mesa. The whole property had been a resort at one time and everything had a clean feel to it. Not a lot of ornamentation, like maybe people came out there to clear their heads. And so much cleaner than a normal set or location.

I thought it was a cowboy picture at first. I figured he hired me as an inside joke because whenever I topped, he called me his cowpoke. But it wasn't like that. The one in the Mojave was a romantic comedy, where a couple of quarreling friends get stuck in a small town when their car breaks down. They were played by fresh faces, up-and-comers who did the kind of vulgar, yet clever stand-up that was in that month. But top billing was a famous old actor. He's one your grandparents would know from the big western TV show you can still order on VHS by the trunkful. How it happens is that these old actor's agents are getting old, too. Maybe they've just got the one client, the old coot from the classic western, and maybe the residual checks are starting to thin. So you make a few calls. Of course in this one, it was different. The famous actor was playing the sheriff, the first good guy role he'd ever done.

It was so breathtaking, the thin dusty air and orange sky out in the Mojave. I'd get up before dawn, hours earlier than the call sheet said I'd have to start. Before the first set up I'd already have had two cups of coffee, and food from craft service, everyone else playing catch-up. And when the time was right, they'd send me in, the Talent Whisperer, the one who mics them up the best because he's done it so many times.

"They're all ready for you," is what I said after I knocked, standing back in the gravel as I was trained to do, to be ready to run in an instant if something explodes.

"You ready for me?" he offered when he opened the door.

"Yes, sir."

He licked his lips the way he did on the old TV show, when he played the bad guy, just before killing someone. Then he just stared. The young men must not have called him sir anymore. Mister So-and-So, or probably not even that.

"What's your name, son?"

"Eddie."

"Eddie what?"

"Eddie Donnelly, sir."

"You mic'ed me up yesterday."

"Yes."

"Well, young Edward, you did a bang-up job. In the old days you'd feel it on you. It tickled and it messed with your head when you did your lines. But I didn't even notice yesterday. It was like I was on stage again, naked as a jaybird."

He stood back and away from the door to let me in. He was in the sheriff's uniform, his beige trousers hung sad and droopy on a frame that clearly didn't hold as much meat as it used to. His six-pointed badge twinkled in the early light and when I stepped fully inside, I could smell his cigarettes and the remnants of the breakfast I'd brought him earlier. Eggs and coffee, and something woodsier, something I didn't bring. Bourbon, perhaps, or rye. His uniform had short sleeves and he held his tanned arms out to his sides to let me work. They were mottled with freckles and wisps of white hair now, but they still had a glimmer of the old game. I thread wires up between his white undershirt and the uniform, a drab polyester number. Like all of us, it was a prop used once too many times. Then, when I was done, I helped him tuck everything back in.

"You're very thorough."

"Thank you, sir."

"You do anything other than this?"

"I can do lots of stuff, sir. Been working on sets since I was a teenager."

"I can tell. You look like someone who really works with his hands out there." He pointed with one chubby thumb in the vague direction of our set. "I like that. You seem to have a solid head on you. That's a good thing to have in this business."

"Thank you."

"How old are you?"

The mechanical whir in the trailer switched over, as though the air conditioning had just stopped running. I felt a little light-headed and took off my baseball cap to wipe my brow.

"Twenty-five, sir."

He whistled. "Quarter-of-a-century man." Something had shifted. His voice dropped into the vaguely Southern drawl he was known for from his old TV show, the one they'd all be expecting him to use on set.

I shrugged as if to say that lots of people are twenty-five nowadays.

"Jake said I should watch for you. Said you're calm as a cucumber. Even when you're fetching, you're focused. Your equipment doesn't even jangle."

"I'm a professional," I said to him, but it made me a little sick as I said it.

"You're all done?"

"You're right as rain," I said. "Ready when you are."

"The mic is off?"

I nodded.

"Lock the door," he instructed and when I'd done it, he tapped at the fake walkie-talkie pinned to his shoulder, a mirror image of the real one pinned to mine.

"Tell them I need a few minutes."

"Of course, sir," I said and radioed it in.

"They copy," I said. "You've got as long as you need. Can I get you anything?"

"Yes," he said and slowly unzipped his pants. He bent forward to give himself the room to reach in and pull out his penis without messing up any part of his fake sheriff's belt. The limp thing dangled there, squat as a sparrow poking its beak from the pleats of his costume.

"What is it you need, Sheriff?" I asked, and the way my voice was so calm, so steady, I was reminded that the old actor was right. I was a professional. I even already knew what his preferences were and, on that day, it was an easy thing to give. How many times with Jake had there been something like this on the side? Something that tripled my day rate. It always began on the fourth day of shooting. Never earlier. You had to get your bearings. You had to save up the moment.

"I can sit over there," I said, pointing to the small bed in the shadows of the trailer where only thin slats of desert light cut their way through the blinds. He nodded.

It would take me only a few minutes to jerk off in those days. I was young and horny and could just lean back and do it. Easy Parcheesi. And when it was some old watcher like that, I didn't even have to think much about him. It was like I was alone. I couldn't see what his hands were doing. Maybe even nothing. The older ones never popped a pill, like Viagra or something, because then you'd have an awkward bulge in your pants all day and the schedule was shot to hell. You never wanted that because then there were conferences in the production trailer and questions from the line producer, and everything got juggled and everyone got angry. A whole set, a whole movie, could unravel like that.

So in the light of that old-school trailer, I pretended Jake was testing me, watching me the way he did my first time. I closed my eyes and saw him there through a break in the blinds.

When I was done and cleaned up, after I'd washed my

hands, we turned on the old actor's mic for real. We did all the tests like normal. He walked around and rustled his shirt and spouted the lines he'd be repeating all day, the ones the whole crew would know by heart and hear in their sleep. He gave a normal delivery, and we tested the levels. It made me happy someplace deep within me to hear those lines, knowing he wasn't the villain this time. He was the good guy with the tobacco grin and a man could live forever in that moment.

THE RULE ABOUT NOT TRUSTING anyone is the one you have to keep the closest, the one you have to cling to when everything else is gone. After the film in the Mojave, Jake skipped town. Rumor was he swindled a producer out of thousands in petty cash and was laying low. I knew it was the tip of the iceberg of what Jake was into. I figured one day I'd get the same treatment, like something out of Raymond Chandler where someone would be knocking on my door to crack wise. Or plug me, shut me up for good. I hear the hard-boiled voiceover in my head: *Too many roads to follow above Sunset, so many strings attached to everyone, you better be careful which ones you pull...*

I holed up with my mom for a long while. She'd quietly gotten her license to be a real estate agent and was hocking property up and down PCH to replace the fortune she'd had and lost. She kept an office at one end of the house and I rarely saw her. I spent long hours planning other businesses, other adventures. Like this one idea about leading a crew of house boys that would clean and keep up the pools of rich Malibu people, even do landscape work. We would build raised beds of vegetables and herbs, so that even if they never used it, they could traipse into their garden, squeeze a handful of rosemary and smell their hand, and feel some connection to the earth.

I took production work here and there. Easy stuff, mostly sound, and with the crews I'd known before Jake. About five years after he disappeared, I took a job corralling talent for a big live network special, the kind they do on big anniversaries when they trot out the cavalcade of stars that used to be on their shows. The special was full of montages and fake-sounding laugh tracks. For the sports segment they flew in the Danish skier that biffed it so bad on the slalom, they've included it on blooper reels since the 1970s. I remember standing in the wings, rehearsal after rehearsal, thinking how sad it is to be remembered only for your most public failure. But mostly the show was upbeat, reuniting beloved casts of the network's most famous comedy and drama series. Minus the one that was written off the show, or the one that always looked sad in the tabloids and died of an overdose.

The famous old actor that did the westerns, the one I'd worked with in the Mojave, he was on the boards all through rehearsals. But his health was failing and the publicist wasn't sure he would actually come. His vision was iffy and he walked with a cane, or so we were told. I would sit in the theater on break, next to the chair on the aisle with his blown-up headshot in it, the kind they set in all the chairs where famous people will be, so the cameras are prepared.

Then at the morning run-through, the day before the show, I heard his voice. I wasn't near the set, but in one of the production trailers. I looked at the nearest monitor to confirm it was him. He looked so much better than I'd imagined—dark jeans and cowboy boots, a red flannel shirt like the ones the kids made hip again, and a large cowboy hat set back high on his forehead. He wore sunglasses inside, dark Ray Bans that made him look like a rock star. His devil grin spread wide as he leaned into the mic.

"Hello," his voice boomed, low and sultry, as though he were saying them just for me.

"You all thought I was dead, and maybe I was," he read, from a piece of paper held close to his face. He lifted his sunglasses up and I could see the cataracts, the pain that had set deep within his face. "But I've come back for you," he finished, with a whisper, the way he sometimes did as the villain on his show.

Later, I found him backstage. He was in a small dressing room, sitting in a chair facing the makeup mirror. He was talking on his cell phone and I stood back in the hallway, waiting for him to finish. His phone looked like an awkward prop in his grip. His wrinkled hand shook a little, but his voice was clear, telling the person what a shit-show they'd gotten him on. "Whole thing takes a minute. They spend more time naming the people who died, for God's sake."

I stepped forward when he was done. He could see me vaguely in the mirror and I looked for a sign of recognition from him, but his eyes had really gone. His vision was stuck in the land of shadows, big ones like those in Monument Valley he'd spent so many years of his life in.

"Can I get you anything?" I asked and when I stepped forward into the room, I noticed to my surprise there was someone else sitting behind him. He couldn't have been older than I was, thirty if he was a day, with cheeks shaved so close and so tan, he looked like someone just in from the islands. He wore a tailored blue suit and rested his head on his hand, causing his sunglasses to go a little askew as he propped one elbow on the counter. He straightened up when he saw me, eyeing me up and down.

"Why Edward Donnelly," the stranger said in a familiar voice.

"Who's that?" the old actor mumbled, confused.

The stranger in the corner stood up and took off his sunglasses. With a degree of horror and shame, I realized it was Jake. Plastic surgery had stretched and smoothed him, but his blue eyes were still cold, the pockets of production stress still rimmed around them.

"I didn't see you on the call sheet, brother," he said, squeezing my shoulders and my arms like a soldier returned from war, seeing how the puppies had grown.

"I'm using a different name now," I said, wishing it wasn't Jake, wishing it was some jerkoff publicist berating me instead, demanding to speak with a producer at once.

"Don't tell me you got *married*," he said, rolling his eyes, but the movement was so strange on his new face, the skin expressionless and taut, that I felt nauseated and faint.

"No, Jake," I said but he put his finger to my lips, holding it there just long enough to tell me he'd gotten a new name now, too. It seemed obvious to me in that moment that all the rumors of his disappearance were true. And that he was high.

"This is *Eddie*," Jake said loudly to the old actor, who was clutching the back of his chair and smiling at us, as though not sure where the familiar face and the unfamiliar one start and end. "You remember him. The comedy a few years back. You played the sheriff."

If the memory made the old actor feel ashamed or excited, it didn't read on his face. "Well I hope I wasn't an asshole. Sometimes I got a mouth on me won't quit."

I didn't know what to say. Here in the bowels of an old Hollywood theater, on set for an anniversary network special, I was suddenly thrust into my own reunion.

"You were terrific," I said, and almost meant it.

"I was, wasn't I?" the old actor said, grinning the devil grin again, the one from his TV show. Although I realized for the first time, being so close to it, that it wasn't a grin at all but a nervous tic, a sign he was anxious or wary, as though he'd breathed in the fumes of his own decay.

I don't remember exactly how I managed to disappear so quickly from that dressing room. It's easy to manufacture a crisis on set, some other place you've got to be. I know I shelved my walkie on the bank of chargers in the production office. I know I left the venue and never looked back.

ON SET, AT THE END of a scene or the end of the day, before moving onto the next location or wrapping out, the sound person always makes everyone stop what they're doing, be quiet, and hold for room tone. They record the ambient noise of the space to be looped in editing, little bridges of sound to cover up any gaps. A necessary magic. The recording might last thirty seconds, a minute. To the crew, it is an interminable pause, an annoyance. For me, it was a meditation, a reset.

I can change my phone number.

I can change my name a second time, try Benjy or Quentin, names from my favorite Faulkner novels, to get out from underneath it all.

And if I ever make my way back to Eddie, I can move someplace new, reset.

A journey.

A stranger comes to town.

JUST HOW I LEFT YOU

Zach Attack prefers our bed when Gary's away and he looks so comfortable there. I know it's cruel to wrench him from that quiet drift atop the sheets, but I've no choice but to take the little guy with me. I've got to get to your house—tonight, in this snow—and see with my own eyes what you've left us.

When I fit on Zach's shoes, he wakes up for a second, squinting at the harsh hallway light, then yawning a singular "Hi, Michael" before falling back asleep. He is Gary's boy, not mine. I'm not a dad to him yet, but I find myself believing I am. I lower his limp body into the backseat of the Bug, wedging him in like Jor-El's superbaby, inside a pod bound for the unknown.

You met Zach only once, at last year's Thanksgiving. He was only six and you had plenty to froth about the little guy then. Zach was just zooming around being Zach, but after Gary's toast you called him the *little shit*. What would you say at the sight of him now, snoozing there in the car you suckered Twigs Ullman out of fifteen summers ago? You'd save the stingers for me, your son pretending to be all grown up, a loser still in between jobs and looking like he never eats, the one stupid enough to be driving your silver Bug through a snowstorm late at night with a boy whose real dad is thousands of miles away. Sit back and toast me with your highball glass of Red Label, bucko. Your son is trekking across the boroughs with nothing on but his chucks, some old jeans, and an over-washed shirt, thinning in the shoulders, which Maggie and I got when we snuck out of your house to see New Order play Hoboken. Listen closely and in the air is a *Fuck you right back, old man*, circa 1980.

I take the Bug up the block, to the end of the cul-de-sac. She squeals to a stop. *I know the way this fox likes her game hen*, you used to say, juicing the car with just enough gas to make it out of the driveway on cold mornings.

Gary hasn't picked up his phone or else I really would have bagged this whole business. His simple drawl and common sense, not to mention the safety of his son, would have slapped me awake by now, but I can't wait. On AM there's a deep female voice, butch and confident, assuring me the plows are out. I don't trust a lot of people, but I trust her. I've plotted a rough course from Larchmont to

Brooklyn. At the light before the expressway, I glance at Zach behind me, watching his arm, long and lanky, scratching at his nose while he sleeps.

The boy has grown a lot in the year since you saw him, maybe even since his dad left last week for the interview. Something in the transition from "Gary's son Zach" to "*our* son Zach" has seeded this growth spurt and his thin arms belie the strength stored within them. We catch him in the backyard throwing rocks over the fence just to see how far he can get them to go. He's only seven, but he'll make a decent pitcher once he gets his aim. I can tell. Zach says he hates baseball. The cocky little bastard sounds like me at that age, calling it boring and too easy.

I can't help but think you'd shake your head at the reason I'm going tonight and not tomorrow or next week when Gary's back. Earlier today, you and your empty house were the furthest from my mind. Zach and I were enjoying our snow day, watching movies and ordering pizza with extra bacon and pineapple, things Gary doesn't like. By two in the afternoon, the boring parts of *Conan the Barbarian* had lulled us into a coma. I woke to the sound of the mail tumbling through the door. Included was the final bill from the Vanderbilt Cleaning Company, the folks who last swept through your house. Maggie hired them and they seemed professional enough, but there was this strange message scrawled in all caps in the notes section of the bill: *LEFT CRATE IN KITCHEN.*

No one answered at the cleaning company when I called. Maggie wouldn't answer her phone either. I read and reread that note a hundred times and all I could hear was your beer-battered breath in my ear, your stubble burning my cheeks telling me *You're not making any sense, say whatchya mean or shut the fuck up already*. Maggie and I lacked focus, you said. We were lazy, you said, *just like your mother*. We were stubborn kids who kept secrets and did bad things. We were disrespectful. Even years after we'd moved out, with our angst softened enough to include you in the birthdays and holidays we thought we all could handle, you always had the right invective for the occasion. *The little shit*, that was the tip of the iceberg. So here you are laughing, wherever you are, as your lazy deadbeat son goes chasing after a stupid crate.

Before I left, I tried putting the thought away. Zach had settled into *Terminator 2*. I microwaved popcorn for him and poured a scotch for me. I tried to focus on the movie, telling myself there was a simple reason for the note and that Maggie would know what it was. In the time it took for the bill to get to me, I was sure she'd already popped over to your place and found the damn thing, something so silly she hadn't even thought to mention it.

But the hours kept clicking by and my mind was looping in on itself with theories of postcards and pilfered photos, theories of your life involving hidden compartments and detailed instructions for some unknown task. I was sweating in our hot little house. My clothes felt too tight and my long hair dirty and tangled. All over I was molting. That stupid note—*LEFT CRATE IN KITCHEN*—filled me with an anger I hadn't felt in a long while, remembering all the fights we had, all the many more I'd imagined in my head.

I locked myself in the bathroom. I stripped and took Gary's trimmer to hack away at all my hair, my shoulder-length curls floating into the tub. I looked dreadful when it was done, my small scalp a shadow of your younger days in boots and fatigues. I showered for a long time to try and put the thoughts of you behind me, but I couldn't. When I came down to put Zach to bed, he screamed at the sight of me. I had changed too quickly for him. He ran away as though he was the Conner boy and I was the T1000 that finally found him. When he finally settled down, I let him watch TV in our bed. And when he was at last asleep—the kid kind of sleep, deep and heavy—I decided to take him with me to your house.

I'd settled into a lane on the expressway behind one of the plows, when Maggie finally picked up her phone. "What are they talking about?" she said. "What crate?" The words seemed to curdle in her mouth and I could picture the cupboard glasses rattling as she poured herself scotch from the old hutch.

"Haven't you been over there? Don't you know?"

"There's nothing left," she said.

251

We'd sorted through the trash of your life. It is hard to believe we'd missed anything not sold, given away or tossed into the dumpster we rented when the realtor told us the carpet and wallpaper had to go. Gary didn't notice anything. Zach might have—he'd find treasure anywhere—but I made sure Zach stayed away. You said it yourself, once: *A dead man's house is no place for a boy.*

"You must have missed something," she said so calmly I wanted to smash my phone on the dashboard. I could hear the tinkle of ice cubes and the bloody mamma music corralling behind her. "Probably some crap in the attic," she said. "Don't worry about it."

"Why would they go up there?"

"Because I *told* them to," she said. "There were cobwebs, remember? You were scared they were going to get tangled up in your stupid hair. Honestly, Michael, cut that mane of yours down before it starts going grey. Are you trying to look like a dirty hippie?" I didn't say that the long Jew locks I inherited from you were already gone.

"What if dad had something up there he didn't want us to find?"

"It worked then, Michael. We didn't find it."

"*Someone* found *something.*"

"They would have called if it was important."

"Maybe they couldn't open it."

"Or it was porn. Honestly, how long do you guys hang on to that shit?"

"It has to be something else."

There was a long silence as she took slurps from her drink. "Maybe he hid some of mom's things," Maggie said, as though she'd thought very hard about how to lay the sentence out.

"You would think anything from mom would have been in that tin we found up in the closet, the one you took with his medal and gun."

"I know it sounds crazy, but maybe there *are* a couple postcards from Montana or some old things of hers. Do you think?"

"Fuck if I know," I said, then silence.

"Is Gary there?"

"He's in San Francisco."

"Where's Zach?"

"With me," I said, looking over at the little dude sleeping in the passenger seat for the umpteenth time.

"*Ohhhhhh*," she said and you know that Maggie can pile a whole lot of bullshit into a word like that.

"Listen, I'll call you when Gary's back and we can go out to the house together," I said. I didn't want to talk about the interview that brought Gary to San Francisco or answer her questions about why Gary was taking another stab at the idea that nearly sunk us last summer. All of that would bleed into what I was doing for work—what I was *not* doing—and all those stupid crazy dreams I had about us moving to California.

"It's going to drive me crazy. I want to go *now*," she slurred, but I had to convince her to stay home, that it was dangerous to take the subway over there at this time of night. I didn't tell her that she always went first. I didn't tell her I was already on my way. I didn't tell her it was my turn now.

I'M MAKING GOOD TIME. I pull off the Westside Highway as it peters out around Chelsea Piers. The island is full of company tonight. At Fourteenth I cut into the West Village, the streets abuzz with young men that the snow and late hour have not deterred. At the wide confluence of Seventh and Christopher and West Fourth, I get stuck at a light. Groups of men huddle in packs around food carts sizzling with bratwurst and roasting cashews. Others stand near the exit to a nightclub, craning their booze-heavy heads for bargains at the sidewalk sale. A few look the way I used to look: glittery eye shadow, bodies shivering in clothes damp with dancehall sweat. When I was younger and you and I came across a group of young men like that—blowing air kisses, telling the world's stories with their hands—you'd make us cross the street. I didn't need to hear what you mumbled under your breath.

The light turns green and Zach Attack belches loudly in my ear, shocking me out of my trance.

"Jesus!" I yell back at him and pull over behind a taxi idling in the slush.

"Where are we going?" he says as he crawls his way into the front seat.

"You *scared* me, Zach." He is surprised to see himself in pajamas and sneakers. He kicks the glove box.

"Can you stop that?"

"Where are we?"

"New York."

He puts his feet down and says, "Where are we *going*?"

"My father's house."

"Why?"

"I need to pick up something."

"What is it?"

"I'm not sure, bucko. You okay?"

Zach shrugs his shoulders and looks outside. Two young men pull at each other's coats, arguing playfully. I watch Zach watch them.

"Put your seatbelt on. Your Game Boy is in the bag—"

"I gotta go pee, Michael."

"Can you hold it? We'll be there in twenty minutes."

"I have to *go*, Michael," he whines. I know there's no fighting this. When I reach Houston Street, I take a quick right and double-park, flipping on the hazards.

"Go right outside the door, okay?"

I get out, too. He is shivering but not yet doing his business. He sees his own breath and so he puffs up his chest and breathes out in a long, steady *huuuuuu*, fists at his sides like he's Superman freezing a river of lava. Gary taught him that trick after we watched *Superman 2*. He's been doing it ever since. Then he grabs a pile of snow from the curb and packs it in his pink hands.

"Would you just go, please!?"

"I don't have to anymore," he shrugs.

"Zach Attack, put that down and try, okay?"

He looks at the forest green Subaru we've parked next to. "Can I go on that car?"

"No."

He places the snowball down gently on the Subaru's bumper, wipes his hands on his plaid flannels and does his business into the snowpack along the curb. He takes forever and hums a song I don't recognize. He makes me feel anxious sometimes, but I can't help but smile when he starts to headbang, jerking his butt around to the rhythm of his mystery song. It's very punk rock. When he finishes, he goes right for the snowball.

"Zach?"

"I won't throw it!"

"I don't care if you throw it. Just don't bring it in the car."

"Really? I can throw it?"

"It's just going to melt," I say before I have a chance to calculate the width of two lanes of traffic and the trajectory of a snowball sent with enough aim and enough force from his taut seven-year-old arm, that it can, and does, splat a white slushy across the door of a Honda four young men have just exited. It has barely missed one of their heads.

"Hey!" yells the tallest one as eight eyes fix themselves on Zach. They know it was Zach because he is laughing. I feel flush. Where are my superpowers now? We've left Krypton, but still I feel weak.

The light changes and the road instantly fills with taxis that block the men in both directions.

"In the car!" I yell and Zach just repeats my name as we scramble with doors and seatbelts. The car stutters, then churns to start and I press hard on the gas. Your old stupid car jerks a little, but then we are free. Two of the men in my rearview are pitching white orbs to the sky. One hits our roof with a whack, the other our hood, but I make turn after turn until I know we've escaped. I want to scream at Zach, but all that comes out is laughter, so hard I'm crying.

"That was close!" Zach keeps saying. No chance he is going back to sleep.

"Where are we going again?" he asks as we get on the Manhattan Bridge. Zach's nose is pressed to the window to look at the buildings, lit up and suspended in fog behind us.

"Brooklyn," I say and his attention's on me again.

"Grimaldi's!?" His vocabulary grows like weeds and Grimaldi's is one of those Brooklyn words he knows. Not Stuyvesant or Flatbush yet, not even the old Dodgers, but he knows Grimaldi's on 19 Old Fulton Street. He can even tell you, in detail, what a pre-war brick oven has to do with the quality of the crust. I love this little man.

"Grimaldi's is closed, bucko. We're going to my dad's place."

"Your dad is dead."

"I know."

"He had a funeral." He says the word *funeral* so perfectly it turns my stomach.

"You were there but you probably don't remember," I say.

"Yes I do! I had to play with Kevin, but he couldn't go in the pool. I wanted to go in the pool. It was hot." He picks at the peeling leather of his door handle.

Vibrating over these steel bridge grates never fails to remind me of you. Here is the stench of your Marlboros, the acrid smell of burnt sugar in the coffee I'm stuck holding for you because Maggie always spills it. Here is Maggie and I stifling a case of the giggles each of the Sunday mornings you drove us to Chinatown for dim sum and fake purse shopping, using us to impress a long line of sad women. Riding the Manhattan Bridge is like riding perfection, something hoisted and sustained by wire, stone and steel, by thousands of ironworkers and engineers, but our trips across it is always too brief.

THIS IS ALSO THE FIRST TIME I've driven this way into Brooklyn—from Manhattan and not the Brooklyn-Queens Expressway—since the last time I saw you alive.

I hadn't planned on seeing you at all, you know. It was

a Saturday in late June. I'd dropped Gary and Zach off at the Botanical Gardens, not far from your house, but I'd driven back to Manhattan to check on a friend at N.Y.U. Hospital. I expected that to eat up all my time before we headed to Yankee Stadium for the game, but my friend already checked out and I had time to kill. Rolling back over those metal grates to Brooklyn, I smelled the same dim sum, the same cheap perfume you bought your lady friends on Canal Street. Those sounds and smells and the fact that I hadn't even spoken to you yet about David Wells pitching a perfect game, all conspired to make me visit you.

I knew enough to stop at Lucky's first to buy you scotch. The man behind the glass stopped watching soccer long enough to see my resemblance to you, staring longer than it took to run my credit card. He probably sold you the stash Maggie and I found in your pantry and the recognition in his eyes made me queasy. I know you only left your house long enough to float in and out of Lucky's, Key Food, and the bank, like you were the neighborhood ghost, haunting all the places you had been the day of the tragedy.

I climbed each step of your narrow brick townhouse, noticing dead weeds in the cracks, shriveled but never removed. I rang the doorbell and through a break in the curtains your shadow lurched and grew. After a long minute, you opened the door a crack before sitting back down. My eyes had to adjust to the room. Only your muted cough placed you where you were sitting, on the couch, between heaps of newspapers.

"Dad?"

You coughed again, louder, and I saw two circles of light where your glasses sat. You mumbled, "Fix us a drink," shifting your weight to one side and knocking over a stack of papers as you fetched inside your jacket for tobacco and a lighter. You were there in the flesh. I've tried so many ways to hate you, or get to other side of that feeling of *wanting* to hate you, for all the ways you hurt us. But you looked so weak and harmless.

When I leaned over to get at the curtains, your firm, familiar hand clutched my shirt.

"Keep 'em closed, Mikey, and fix us a drink."

"Okay," I said. "But I'm turning on something."

On my way to the kitchen, I pulled the chain on the lamp atop the old upright, and the light buzzed in its green frame. In your cluttered living room, I was unable to see it as it once had been, with the large picture window lit up with a December spruce, Maggie stabbing carols into the keys. We'd always been the worst Jews on the block, trading Christmas presents because it reminded you of mom. But all that was gone. Now there was just you, teetering on the edge of the couch as precariously as your newspaper clippings.

I rinsed two highball glasses, sensing a quiet sterility to your kitchen. Few odors lingered except coffee grounds and lemon soap. Perhaps an infestation of mice or roaches had prompted things to be bleached and sprayed, cracks caulked and holes stuffed with high-grade steel wool. I thought your kitchen had been singled out to remain ageless, a panic room where light never penetrated enough to fade the wallpaper and there would always be canned food.

"I left a message," I lied, handing you a glass and clearing a place to sit.

"I said *scotch*," you growled and there it was, the old familiar bark.

"It *is*."

"This is *soda watah*," you said, slipping into your old Brooklyn accent. You drank it down anyway and jangled your ice at me. I poured you a second with less soda, less ice.

"They'd install cameras to watch me all day if they could. Don't think that fucker across the street hasn't thought about it. He shoots at me, you know. For fun, he shoots up my back lawn. I seen him do it."

"You call the cops?"

"They don't care. They talk to that shyster over there, but they don't do a goddamn thing. I talked to one of them, but they all think I'm incompetent. I'm not incompetent. It's *them* that come in here and climb over *my* fence and shoot up *my* lawn."

You took a long gulp of your scotch. It calmed you.

"Maggie know you're here?"

"No," I said. Then you pointed your mottled, withering hand at me as though ringing an imaginary doorbell.

"Why you got a Yankees cap on your head?"

"Why not?" I'd forgotten I was wearing it.

"You don't like baseball."

"I like it enough. Gary and I are taking Zach to the game today."

"Oh. David Wells is pitching, you know. Don't expect that fat fuck to give you the pleasure this evening. Lightning don't strike twice."

I caught sight of the framed newspaper clipping by the door, the one of Sandy Koufax.

"Koufax had a couple games where he did that."

"No hitters, Michael! He had three no hitters, but only one perfect game. Only one."

I expected you to list the usual details. The summer of 1965. Palm trees at the grove by Olvera Street downtown. Killing time before the game. You and Aunt Wendy sitting cross-legged and enjoying the mariachi band, feeling the sweet sting of horchata on your fillings. Crossing Echo Park in the blue Thunderbird and making your way to Dodger Stadium. You always took us through the double header play-by-play, building up to that eerie quiet in the final innings. The Dodger Dogs and beer ate away at your stomach and you were so nervous for Koufax you thought you'd throw up. You loved to imitate Vin Scully's nasally pitch as he called the final out:

> *Swing on and missed! A perfect game! On the scoreboard in right field it is 9:46 p.m. in the*

*City of the Angels, Los Angeles, California,
and a crowd of twenty-nine thousand and one-
hundred thirty nine just sitting in to see the only
pitcher in baseball history to hurl four no-hit,
no-run games. He has done it four straight years,
and now he capped it: on his fourth no-hitter, he
made it a perfect game!*

That is what I expect from you, reliving that game, getting worked up as you describe the Dodgers rushing onto the field to pile Koufax at the mound, after you and every other fan stood and clapped for a lifetime. You and your sister float like pinwheels to the car and drive Sunset all the way to the ocean. You wade into the Pacific and tell Wendy your dream to move your pregnant wife and daughter out west. You gulp the Santa Ana winds blowing down the bluff, you say you wish your family could be stuck in a box and shipped there overnight. You're so in love, you ship California back to Brooklyn. You buy loads of oranges and lemons, coconut tanning oils and a special skin cream Wendy told you all the actresses used. You ship it east in large crates that arrive for days after you are back.

But you and mom never made it west. You and mom and little Maggie ate up as much as you could, watching most of it spoil. Mom had me and not long after, she left us. I know it was only too easy for the California dream to burrow itself into you while you were there. I know that now. It was perfection to you, every smell, every bite of fruit, every drop of tequila. Even the baseball was perfect.

From that same spot on your couch, you'd told me that story a million times, growing from quiet to angry to tears in a matter of minutes. But I realized then, in your silence, that the fire within was running out of oxygen. The structure was toppling in on its embers. It was always so easy to fight with you and yet I didn't have it in me anymore with you like that.

"You bringing them by, I suppose?" you asked, staring at a spot of sun on the carpet as though the consonants you'd lost could be found there.

"No," I said, "Not since Thanksgiving." You had never liked any of my boyfriends, least of all Gary and his son. When I was younger, I'd still bring them to you. I liked rubbing it in your face. I liked being the man you couldn't cross the street from. And I always stuck around so you could drink me under the table and say the vile things that had been on your mind—Nick was an *AIDS fucker* because he worked on Broadway, Jay was a *faggot cop,* and Rudy, well, Rudy was a twofer: the *wetback queen.*

Gary and Zach have gotten off easy I have to admit.

"They're not coming here," I said, as if to make sure I believed it. But I couldn't help what came out of my mouth next. "I've got the car," I said. "We can drive over to the park, if you'd like. There's plenty of time before the game."

You shifted in your seat. You considered it.

"No, Michael," he said, so softly I barely heard it. "You go and have fun at the game."

"Are you sure? What do *you* want?" I asked, feeling like I'd never asked you that.

"I don't want anything." Your coughing ramped up, fiercer than ever. I realized you did want something. You wanted me to leave. You wanted me to keep Gary and Zach away from you, from whatever poison caused you to spray the drive and bleach the counters, whatever vermin made you stuff the walls with steel wool.

I got up and opened the front door, waiting for you to say something else. I stared again at the little framed newspaper photo of Koufax you have hanging on the strip of wall by the door. He is young, mid-career, winding up for a fast pitch in faded yellow newsprint. Why you tortured yourself with that memory I'll never know.

You didn't say a word. I walked back over to you and kissed your scaly forehead. One simple peck. You looked up at me, staring into my eyes which are the same as yours. You squeezed my arm so tight, I winced. Then at last you balked and your grip loosened forever.

ZACH SIGHS DEEPLY AS I pull off the Prospect Expressway.

"Just a little further," I say.

"What did you forget there?"

"I'm not sure anymore."

The snow has picked up a bit and the streets have

accumulated more snow than those in Manhattan, much more than the roads back home when we left.

"Which house is it?" he asks. The brick row houses on Howard Place look identical, save for the details that are hard to see in the dark.

"Third on the right," I say, then "the one with the lights still on."

Standing on the porch, we can see Maggie through the window. She sits cross-legged by the fireplace, blazing up one *Village Voice* after another. Her eye makeup is streaked down to her cheeks, which are pink and swollen. She is still your daughter, still my pudgy punk mess of a sister.

I grab Zach's hand and slip the key in the door, startling Maggie.

"Michael!" she says, trying to get up, but falling further backward instead. I see a large emerald bottle that's rolled into the corner.

"What are you doing? Wow! You really chopped off your hair. I was only joking. Jesus, you look like—oh, hi Zachary."

Zach says "Hi" under his breath. Whatever energy he's had tonight, it's been sucked out by the fire and the sight of Maggie. His face pushes into my side.

"You came all the way here with *him*?" she says, bracing herself to stand again.

"Did you find the crate? What is it?"

"It's in the kitchen, just as the man said. *Left crate in*

kitchen!" She says this like she's a cavewoman.

I whisper to Zach, "Go sit by the fire and warm up, okay?"

"I want to go with *you*."

"Sit by the fire and don't touch anything. We're not staying long."

"But—?"

"I can see you're cold. I'm cold, too. Just sit there for a second and we'll go soon."

The empty room seems large with nothing but Zach in it, but he sits by the fire and holds his hands up the way he thinks you're supposed to, rubbing them a little against each other and then up to the warm grate.

Maggie takes me by the arm and waltzes me to the kitchen. She flips on the bare bulb.

I don't believe what you've left us. We have seen and tripped over this crate hundreds of times. We have stood on it, leveraged it for newspaper as we wrapped your kitchenware for Goodwill. We never pried it open. We never let ourselves dwell on its contents. Of course we knew its branded logo by heart: a sun setting over distant hills and the cursive *Santa Barbara, CA* etched on its side. We knew its dimensions—two feet square at the base and fourteen inches tall—because that had been part of your story, too, the maximum size that would fit inside the coat closet of the plane. You fought with the stewardess about it and won because no one brought coats to California. We knew the crate's contents—four large bottles of champagne—and we knew why they'd been saved. One bottle was to be broken on the prow of the Buick when you set off for California, the second to be drunk when your feet touched the Pacific again. The last two were for us, uncorked when Maggie and I each turned twenty-one. But that legend died a long time ago.

There is no table in your kitchen—no island either. Since the countertops are too narrow, the crate sits awkwardly on the floor, its packing hay, stale and strong, strewn every which way.

"The big reveal!" Maggie says, "Stick that in your plot and smoke it!"

"We gave that away!"

"I didn't," Maggie says with a shrug. "I thought you did."

There is something else she's found and hasn't said. She is a horrible liar. Feeling dizzy—how long since I've eaten anything?—I grab the doorframe and look behind me. Zach stares back but doesn't say anything. The emerald bottle lying on its side catches a reflection of the fire. Your daughter has already chugged clean through the first one. But what else is there?

I breathe in deeply and move toward the crate. I prop up one of the last three bottles. It's dusty and dirty, glowing green where my damp fingers touch it. I run my hand across its face to see the label. The words are mostly French, *cuvee* this and *fleur* that, but the address in Santa Barbara is clear, as is the vintage.

"I think it's a sign," Maggie says. "He wants us to find her, to find out what happened. He kept it because he kept hope." Another one of your storms lands ashore in her eyes. I realize Maggie hasn't found anything else, no note, no secret stash of photographs. There isn't anything else. This crate alone is going to send her down the rabbit hole. Me, too, if I let it.

I palm the bottle and feel its weight. I will take just one with me. I will wash it off and open it with Gary when he gets home, but we'll make no ceremony for you. I won't take that journey the way Maggie will. This is all you've left us and I realize you were right. Zach must get far away from here.

I turn to find my son, but he's already standing right behind me. I collide with him and all the energy in my bones releases itself. The bottle slips from my hands and shatters wildly at our feet. The sound pops our ears so all that's left is the hiss of bubbles burrowing into floorboards.

"Fuck," I yell, trying to grab Zach and keep him from stumbling.

Zach freezes, eyes wide. "Don't move," I say, but he can't help it. He takes a step backward to get away and slips on a large piece of glass, falling backward and landing hard on the floor.

"Oweeeeeeeeeeeee!" he screams. I sit him up, checking

his back, his butt, everywhere for blood, for signs that somehow your house got him and got him good. There are no gashes, no wounds, only scrapes raised up in rows on his arms that match the floor's unpolished, splintery wood.

Zach and I take a deep breath together. I brush glass from his pajamas. He stifles his sobs, rubs his fist against his eyes and doesn't protest when I kiss his head. I lift him up and sit him on the counter next to the sink. Maggie is there in the room, but I pretend she's not and Zach tries not to look at her because she scares him. The pipes clang and specks of brown water spurt out, until finally there's a steady stream clear enough to wash Zach's arm.

"It hurts, Michael," he says, his attention on his arm now, on me.

"I know, bucko. Let's go outside and get some snow for that."

He nods and wraps his arms around my neck. I carry him past a stunned and silent Maggie, past the rooms that smell like they're vomiting champagne.

Maggie follows us to the porch. Does she think I'm going to hurt him? I stand him up against the railing and gently hold a little snow to the reddest strips of his forearm. He flinches at the cold and then giggles.

"It's not so bad," she slurs. "We'll wrap it up and you'll be asleep before you know it."

I tear my thin t-shirt off into two strips. The frigid air races up my sweaty back, making my teeth chatter, but I don't care. I cup some snow and twist it into one of the strips and have Zach hold it against his arm. We shiver together, but he looks up and smiles. It's as close to a perfect game as I'm going to get.

"There, see?" Maggie says, leaning against the bay window and lighting a cigarette. "Uncle Michael made it all better."

I bristle at the word *uncle* and stare at my sister, your daughter, wishing I could reach down her throat and wrench your ugly word from her lips.

"I gotta go," I say, picking Zach up for the last time and carrying him to the car. The wind bites at my arms, my neck. I have never been so cold.

"He's fine, Michael. Don't freak out. Just stay with me a little while!" Maggie shouts back. I put Zach inside Jor-El's space pod, setting our course for anywhere beyond this dying planet. He pulls the blanket over his head. I rub his hair and close his door. I look at your house for the last time. Maggie stands on the porch, holding one of the two remaining bottles out to me.

"Take it!" she howls into the otherwise peaceful Brooklyn night. She double-steps it down the porch and up the drive. I shake my head and hurry into the Bug. *I know the way this fox likes her game hens.* Maggie is at my window and I crack it open just enough to hear.

"Take the bottle," Maggie says.

"I don't want it."

"It's a sign, Michael. You've got to take it—"

"You go and look for whatever you need, Maggie. We're leaving." What I mean is that I'm leaving, to California, with Gary and Zach, but I don't say that because I have never said it out loud. It is that fragile. It is an ancient bone I'm dusting off, something so small and delicate that Maggie, like you, would be only too happy to stomp on it.

"We're moving to California," I say after all, but Maggie doesn't hear over the engine and I don't repeat it. But Zach has heard me.

"I'm sorry, Zach," she shouts, pressing her lips to the cracked window, "I hope you feel better." Then she steps away as I pull out. I don't look back.

My teeth are still chattering when we pull into the empty Key Food parking lot, a block from the onramp.

"Does it still hurt?" I ask, looking back at him.

He shrugs. I want to believe he is thinking about California, like I am.

"You have two choices. We go see a doctor now or we go home."

He looks at his arm. There is no sign of my shirt with the snow in it, just the scratches beaded with a little blood. "Home," he says.

When we're back on the expressway, he pokes my side with his foot.

"You're skinnier than dad," he says.

"I know."

"And taller."

"Yeah," I say. "Your dad's a pipsqueak."

"Rodney's older brother is really tall. He plays basketball. Did you ever play basketball?"

"No way," I say, laughing.

He's laughing, too. He sounds like Gary, with those low dorky guffaws. On our careful ride home, Zach never falls asleep. He talks and talks, never asking for his Game Boy. When he unbuckles and climbs to the front seat, I don't tell him no. He asks me about every sport he can think of and when he finally gets to baseball, I don't think at all before telling him about the perfect game. I explain twenty-seven up and twenty-seven down. I tell him how out of all the tens of thousands of games since baseball was invented, that there have been only maybe twenty perfect games. I tell a quick version of your story, Dad, about the perfect game in '65, about Sandy Koufax. I build up to the final inning, saying just what Vin Scully said when he called it, that the mound at Dodger Stadium right then was the loneliest place in the world.

Zach ponders this a minute. "I like that story," he says.

At Gary's house, the driveway needs shoveling and the electric garage door won't budge. I park sideways into a bank of snow. Zach lets himself out and runs through the snow to the porch. Inside, to our relief, the house is still warm. Zach races upstairs.

"You need to change your clothes," I call after him, making it slowly up the steps.

"Are we really moving to California?" he shouts from his room.

"Yes, bud! To San Francisco" I shout back, smiling that the idea has taken root.

"You and me and Dad?"

"You and me and Dad."

ACKNOWLEDGMENTS

To the Full Frontal Writing Collective who keep me in the chair each week: my partner in crime and cofounder Beth Heald, and fellow mischief-makers Elizabeth Lahti, Kathryn Lipari, and Michael Szporluk—thank you for all the Wednesday nights.

To Write Around Portland, for your clear mission and all you've taught me about writing in community. To Literary Arts, for your financial support and to the incomparable Kates (Gray and Carroll de Gutes) for creating and hosting the Incite: Queer Writers Read series, giving us a platform and a means to connect. And to the many queer journals and their editors who put faith in my fiction, flash, and poetry.

To the friends, artists, and teachers I've been blessed to talk about words with and be inspired by since landing in Portland, a waterfall of thank yous to Sara Guest, Liz Scott, and Robert Hill, as well as Alex Behr, Ben Moorad, Brian Padian, Donnella Wood, Emme Lund, Hana Layson, Heidi Greenwald, Jan Baross, Jen Stady, Jennifer Lalime, John Forsgren, John Morrison, Kate Cox, Kathleen Lane, Kathy Lawrence, Kristin Bacon-Brenes, Lesley Painter, Liz Eslinger, Lyne Martin-Modica, Margaret Malone, and Robyn Steely.

To the Fuck You Thank You sangha, to family, friends, neighbors, and fellow city employees who have supported me on this path.

To the best editor and friend a writer could have, Jerry Sampson, without whom this book wouldn't exist. And to Buckmxn for putting their faith in these stories.

Finally, to my husband Jonathan, who makes me a better writer through his honesty, integrity, and bright humanity. We lowered the cliff together.

Stacy Brewster is a fiction writer, poet, and screenwriter. Born in Los Angeles and raised both there and in the San Francisco Bay Area, he studied filmmaking in New York and has since worked in television, independent film, advertising, publishing, politics, and public service. His fiction and poetry have appeared in *New South*, *The Madison Review*, *Plenitude*, and *The Gay & Lesbian Review Worldwide*, among numerous others. He was awarded the 2019 Oregon Literary Arts Fellowship in Drama for his teleplay *Gargoyles & Dandelions*, an as-yet-unproduced one-hour queer noir series set in Los Angeles in the late 1940s.

Due to chronic neuropathy, Stacy uses assistive dictation software to aid him in writing. He has facilitated writing workshops for seniors and people with disabilities and also lectured on the intersection of disability and creative practice. He works as a copy editor in Portland, Oregon and lives there with his partner (now husband) of nearly two decades, Jonathan, and their dog Lucinda. This is his first book.

CPSIA information can be obtained
at www.ICGtesting.com
Printed in the USA
BVHW040921231121
622333BV00017B/531

9 781733 724548